GIVE ME DESIRE - REASON SERIES #3

Zoey Derrick

GIVE ME DESIRE - REASON SERIES #3

Zoey Derrick

Cover Designer: Parajunkee. Www.parajunkee.net Thank you so much Rachel for all your amazing hard work for The Reason Series and all the lovely images that accompany your amazing covers.

Editing: The Editing of The Reason Series has been completed by Sione Aweschliman of Sione Aeschliman LLC. Thank you Sione for all your hard work.

To my Beau - You've been there for me, through everything. I heart you & miss you!

The entire Reason Series is dedicated to all the men and women around the world who are or have been a victim of Domestic Violence.

A Little Reminder

Because we all need one from time to time:

Chapter 46 - Give Me Hope:

The room has been completely silent for a while, and the loud click of the door makes us both jump. Looking toward the door, we see Dr. Alston coming into the room.

"Am I interrupting?" she asks both of us.

"No," we say in unison, and Vivienne smiles, giving me hope that she's not upset with me.

Dr. Alston laughs. "Well, okay then. Vivienne, I have some good news."

"Yay! Do I get to get out of here?"

"I'll get to that. First of all, your shoulder and wrist look great. I will let you take off the sling, but I'd like you to wear the brace for at least another couple of days. You can take it off to shower, but put it back on when you're done. Okay?"

"Okay, is that all?"

"Eager, aren't we?" Dr. Alston smiles at Vivienne. "Your lung is still healing. While the outside is nearly completely healed, which is nothing like anything I've ever seen before, it's still a bit inflamed. But it's nothing that will keep you here in the hospital."

"What about the baby?" I ask, and Vivienne looks to me for reassurance.

I move closer to her, hoping to provide a little more comfort, and she surprises me by putting her hand on my back. I feel a rush of pleasure through my body that has to do with something more than the fact that she is touching me, and I realize that she is tracing her fingers absently along my right wing. When her fingers cross over to normal skin, the difference in the sensation is marked.

"The baby is doing fine. You're measuring a little bigger than fourteen weeks, but clearly that's due to the fact that you've been eating more food." She looks pointedly at the remains of Vivienne's sandwich on the tray. "What with the unnatural rate at which you're healing, I'm not going to be concerned right now about weight.

"Also...I didn't ask you during the ultrasound because I didn't want to get you worked up, but I was able to determine Baby Callahan's sex, and I've taken the liberty of putting the proof in here." She pulls out an envelope from her pocket. "I've never been wrong," she says a little smugly, "but it's not guaranteed. And I'd rather you look when you're ready to find out. If you choose not to look, well, it will be a surprise when you have the baby."

"Okay," Vivienne says, taking the envelope. "I'll let you know next time whether I've decided to look. Now can I leave?"

Dr. Alston rolls her eyes. "So impatient." Then she asks, "Where are you going to go?"

My ears perk up and my heart sinks, dreading the answer.

"I can't discharge you unless I know you're going somewhere safe," Dr. Alston continues. "Hospital policy. Do you have something set up?"

She nods.

I grow hopeful that she will take me up on my offer.

"Mikah has offered me a place to stay for a while, until I can get back to work and on my feet. I'm going to go home with him."

YES! I shout inside my head, and at the same time Vivienne gently pats my back, right between my shoulders. I have the sudden thought that Vivienne has been in my dreams with me.

"I think that is a great idea. I've scheduled an appointment for you for two weeks from tomorrow at ten. And no working at least until then, okay?"

"Yes, ma'am."

"Okay, here are your discharge papers." She hands Vivienne a stack of papers. "You cannot walk out of this hospital – it is a liability – but someone will come with a wheelchair to get you in a little bit. That'll give you a chance to get packed up, and then that's it, you're free to go."

"Thank you, Dr. Alston. For everything."

"You're welcome, Vivienne. It's what I'm here for. I rather look forward to seeing you under happier circumstances. I will be in touch in a couple of days to see how you're doing. I'll see you in a couple of weeks, but feel free to call me if you need anything before then."

As soon as the door closes behind Dr. Alston I turn to Vivienne. "Thank you. For not putting up a fight about my request."

She lets out a breathy laugh. "Yeah, 'cause you gave me so many options. But in the end, you're right, I really have no place else to go, and I'd much rather be closer to you."

I lean over and kiss her forehead. "Thank you, thank you, thank you."

"For what?"

"Giving me hope."

Prologue

"Do not toy with me." His anger radiates off him in waves and the temperature in the room rises.

"It is done, Master. I've completed the task you've assigned me." He does not look upon the other man's face as he speaks. He's kneeling some distance away, causing him to shout to be heard.

"Get up!" The evil voice fills the room, stunning everything inside.

The young man stands but does not raise his head.

The scene changes, and instead of a small, dark room, they are in a cavernous one, with strange pockets of steam rising through cracks in the rock floor. Somewhere nearby echoes of the hollow screams of tortured souls can be heard.

"Your job was simple, you were to kill her. Here you stand, not only her blood but the blood of at least two others on you. And yet I do not believe you have completed your task, minion. Why is this?"

"I don't know. I left her dead, she was dead when I left." He begins mumbling – low and incoherently - and twitches as though he can't stand his own skin.

"Ah, but she is not dead. If she were dead, I'd have all my powers back, and..." Suddenly the room is lit up by a bright white flash. The air is instantly charged, static making hair stand on end, and the young man crumples to the ground. "And I'd be able to kill you."

"No! Don't. Don't hurt him," a female voice says, and a girl runs from behind a rock to be at the young man's side.

"Who are you?" the dark, mysterious man shouts.

"What are you doing to him?" She looks down at the crumpled form on the floor and reaches out to touch his dirty blond hair. Looking up in the direction of the voice. "Who are you?"

A deep, throaty laugh comes from the man in the shadows, making the hairs on the back of her neck stand to attention. "I am your worst nightmare, child."

The echo of heavy footsteps across the rock floor fills the cave, each step getting closer. She cowers, trying to pull the young man with her, but she fails. She lets him slump to the ground as she scrambles backwards on her hands and feet.

"What are you going to do to me?" she whispers breathlessly. Her body shakes in fear.

There is no response as the shadowy figure keeps walking closer with slow, measured steps.

"It is not you I wish to harm, child. It is this boy who needs a lesson in obedience." There is an edge of reverence in his voice, as though he's longing for something.

"What are you going to do to him?" she asks, the fear dropping away from her voice.

"If he'd done what he was supposed to do, I'd do nothing to him. But he has failed me and he deserves to be punished, perhaps tortured." The voice is menacing and yet also strangely enticing to her.

"Take me instead," she says, and she rises to her feet.

The footsteps stop. "What would I want with you, girl?"

"Anything, everything. Let Riley go and take me instead."

"Tell me your name, child." It comes out a growl.

"Nyssa."

ONE

Vivienne

I feel amazing, but why?

I look around, but there is nothing to see, nothing to look at, but solid white. Am I dead?

"No, darling, you are very much alive."

I spin around, trying to find the source of the gentle female voice, but I see nothing more than the white walls surrounding me.

"Who are you?" My voice is calm, but inside anxiety spikes at the unfamiliar voice.

"I'm here to help guide you," the voice says. It is soft, gentle and reassuring, but I'm still confused. "Someone is waiting for you down that hallway behind you."

I turn around hastily and am momentarily thrown off balance. *Oh yeah, my wings*, I think, as though I've had them my entire life, and flex my shoulders. A part of my mind – the part that knows I've never had wings – finds it odd that I'm so unconcerned about it.

After a moment, I regain my balance and begin heading down the hallway, and my heart starts to pound at the idea of what's waiting for me at the end.

As I'm walking, I take a look down at my dress. It's soft and white, with silver beads along the bodice in an intricate design below my breasts. My chest looks bigger - a lot bigger - than I remember, but looking down beyond them I can see why.

Standing out in perfect roundness is my baby bump, no longer a bump but very much a pregnant belly. I stroke it absently and note the silver, cuff-like bracelet around my wrist, its beautiful Celtic design highlighted by a shiny white stone in the center. The cuff extends down the back of my hand almost to my knuckle with its very detailed design.

Then I realize that there is also something cool pressing against my forehead. I can't see it, and when I try to pull on it, it tugs at my hair, so I leave it alone. It feels like a tiara or some type of headpiece.

I keep walking further down the hall; it's long and narrow, with no end in sight. I can't imagine how big this place is with a hall this long. My feet make no sound against the floor and I realize that I'm barefoot.

After a few moments more, I see something up ahead. A figure. I can't make out the details, but a rapidly growing longing churns inside me, and I quicken my pace.

But no matter how far I go, I just can't quite get there. Frustration boils. I'm reminded of a never-ending nightmare and my heart rate increases with unease.

Finally the figure comes into better focus. It's a man, shirtless and sporting an intricate black tattoo along his right shoulder and down his right arm. His skin has a nice tan tone to it against all the white behind him and the white pants he's wearing. His black hair is tousled as though he's been sleeping. Seeing the image as a whole sends a jolt of desire throughout my entire body. Every nerve is alive with an urgent need to be close to him.

And then an undercurrent of fear washes through me as the idea that I could need or want someone this much washes through me. I've never desired anyone before.

Mikah? I ask myself. Could it really be him? What is he doing here? How did he get here?

The wings, the fact that I don't know that I've ever felt this good in my life...this has to be heaven; there is no other explanation for it, despite what I was told earlier. But if I'm in heaven, what is Mikah doing here? And does this mean I'm dead?

That female voice from earlier returns in the same friendly tones as before. "You are not in heaven, my dear. You are in Elysium, a place where only a few chosen are allowed to travel. Your presence here has nothing to do with being dead. You are very much alive."

"Who are you?" I ask again.

"My name is Zirah, and I am your guide."

"Guide for what?"

"I am here to help you understand all the changes your body is going through. Mainly, I'm here to help you understand that you, my child, are a Chosen. You are an angel."

Suddenly the view in front of me shifts. The room is an ominous grayish-black. I blink a few times, adjusting to the dark after the stark white of a few moments ago.

There is a bright flash up ahead that lights up the room, and I hear a girl scream. Picking up my skirt, I run as quickly as I can manage on the rocky floor. A hot flame arcs across my back, and my wings twitch. I look over my shoulder, but there is nothing there. The flame grows hotter but is not yet painful as I approach the place where the flash of light came from.

"What would I want with you, little girl?"

"Anything, everything. Let Riley go and take me instead."

"What is your name, child?" The deep, menacing voice echoes through the cavern.

"Nyssa."

TWO

"Vivienne.... Vivienne, come on. Wake up."

That voice. I...I know him. I know that voice.

"Come on, sweetie. It's time to go home."

What?

My eyes begin to flutter open. I see his eyes – blue and green mixed to create the most beautiful effect that mimics the ocean – and they are warm, caring...and there is something else in them that I can't name.

"There you are," he whispers. "You were having a nightmare."

I can feel my mouth make that O shape, but nothing comes out.

"It's alright, you're safe."

I blink a couple of times, trying to shake the dream I was having and bring myself back into the present. Instinctively I know what I was hearing, but how? Why? Why me? Why was Nyssa in my dream? I couldn't see her, but is it possible that it really is the Nyssa I know? Instinct tells me that it is.

"Hi," I grumble sleepily to Mikah.

He smiles at me. "Hi. You ready to go?"

I nod my head. My neck, though I've played it off, is still a little sore. I've managed not to look in the mirror, but for as much pain as I was in when it happened, my arm doesn't hurt at all. I've finally ditched the sling, but Dr. Alston is making me keep the brace on my wrist. It seems utterly pointless, but I'm not going to argue anymore.

An orderly comes into the room pushing a wheelchair. At least this one doesn't have the stupid yellow flag on top of the pole like the one earlier did.

I let out a sigh. I get to leave the hospital, but I've capitulated to Mikah's demand to take me back to his apartment – or rather to a different one originally meant for his housekeeper, Celeste. A part of me wonders whether or not he'll actually let me stay in that apartment or whether he'll try to convince me to stay in his.

But the fact remains: The longer I thought about whether or not to go with Mikah, the more I realized that I couldn't come up with any rational reasons to not go. Riley is still on the loose, and no matter where I go, he can always search for me. The idea of Mikah getting hurt makes my heart constrict, but Red will be there, too.

Furthermore, Dr. Alston and Nurse Fang – Amanda – have told me that I can't work again until after I see Alston in a couple of weeks, which means I can't afford my apartment anymore.

My apartment. It suddenly dawns on me Mikah is right: I won't ever be able to go back there again. The memories are too horrible, and I know that I'd never feel safe there again. But I also know that there are things there that I want.

I turn to Mikah as he helps me get down off of the hospital bed and whisper, "I need to go back to my apartment first. My stuff," I say, not wanting to display the fear I'm feeling about going back there.

His eyes widen a fraction. "What's in your apartment that you need?" he asks.

"My journal, my clothes, and the picture you gave me." My breath hitches at the idea of my baby's ultrasound picture.

Mikah stiffens at the mention of the picture. His eyes take on a very distant, thoughtful look, almost as though he is trying to recall something. "Where are the picture and your journal?"

"The picture is next to my bed, and the journal is under the foot of the bed, wedged between the pallet and the mattress."

He doesn't respond but rather reaches for his phone as he helps me sit in the wheelchair. He presses a button and puts it to his ear.

"Are you ready to go, Ms. Callahan?" the orderly behind me asks.

"I just need my stuff."

I spot a rather expensive duffle bag sitting at the foot of the bed.

"Red, can you go to Vivienne's apartment and collect a picture and her journal?"

"What about my clothes?" I say as Mikah reaches for the bag. He holds up one finger.

Slinging the duffle over his shoulder, he looks to the man behind me. "Let's go." But he hasn't said anything to Red about my clothes. "When did you do that?" he says into the phone. "Oh, okay then. Wait, what about the picture?" My heart sinks as Mikah's face falls. "I'll tell her. Thanks, Red."

He pulls the phone from his ear, presses a button, then puts it back to his ear as he walks alongside me, not giving me a chance to say anything.

"Celeste, we're leaving the hospital now. Were you able to take-" He cuts off.

"Perfect, thank you. We'll be home shortly. I'm going to take her downstairs." He pauses. "Okay, thanks."

We stop in front of the elevators. As Mikah pulls the phone away from his ear, the orderly hits the down arrow and I turn toward Mikah. "What about my picture?" I say. My tone is clipped, irritated.

Mikah's eyes dart to mine; they're wary. "The picture was gone when Red went by your apartment last night."

My heart sinks. I loved that picture. But where could it have gone? Why is it gone? Did Riley take it?

"Celeste already ordered a new frame, same as the other one. It should be here by Tuesday. And I still have the original picture, so I can replace the image."

"Thank you," I say quietly, still contemplating where the photo could've gone in the first place.

"You're welcome." He smiles. "Red took care of your apartment. Cleaned it up and moved all your stuff to the condo."

I nod, relieved that I don't have to deal with it myself but still sorry to see the apartment and my independence go, at least for now.

We ride the elevator down in silence. As we approach the entrance of the hospital, through the glass doors I see a limo parked in front of the door. I can't tell, but I'm pretty sure that it is the same one from a couple weeks back. We come through the double doors and there are two men standing on either side of the car, both very tall with broad shoulders. One has bright red hair, similar in color to my own, but in a short military cut. The other has darker hair, also cut short, but not as short as the first one's.

My heart rate increases and anxiety flares as we come through the door. The one with red hair moves to the back door of the limo and opens it. Mikah hands him the bags, and he moves around to the trunk. My nerves settle a little as understanding registers: These are more of Mikah's men.

As Mikah extends his hand to me, I catch the orderly's movement in the corner of my eye. I flinch, panic washing through me, and I jerk away from him. He reaches for the wheel lock on the chair. On my other side, I can see Mikah's hand, but I'm frozen in place. Then I realize all the orderly is doing is securing the wheelchair.

"Vivienne," I hear Mikah say quietly, and I turn stiffly in his direction. He mouths, "It's okay." I feel the fear wash out of me and I place my hand in his.

Stepping out of the wheelchair, I'm steadied by Mikah, who says to the orderly, "Thank you."

"Have a safe trip home," the orderly replies and wheels the empty chair back into the hospital.

THREE

Mikah leads me to the door of the limo and urges me to climb in. My hesitation to do so doesn't go unnoticed by him.

"Andrew?"

"Sir?" the dark-haired one replies.

"Can you hit the interior lights and roll down the windows?" Mikah asks him.

I try but fail to smile at Mikah's quick thinking.

"Yes, sir," Andrew says, and I watch as the interior lights come on and the windows go down. I even catch motion in the top as the sunroof opens.

"Thanks," I say so only Mikah can hear me.

"Of course." He starts again to help me into the limo, and this time I go a little more freely, as I can see everything inside. "If you sit up toward the front, you won't be as cold."

I clamber up to the small bench seat, not at the front but on the driver's side, and I sit down.

Mikah follows behind me, taking the seat next to me, his back to the driver. I shiver slightly as the colder air registers, and he puts out his arm. I slide closer to him and rest my head on his shoulder. In a slow, calculated move he brings his hand down so that his arm is along my back and his hand is on my hip. Holding me to him, he lightly kisses the top of my head.

We ride in silence, me fighting heavy eyes as exhaustion tries to consume me. I close my eyes but don't fall asleep.

I replay my dream - the one in the white hallway - trying hard to make sense of it.

I felt so alive, so free, and yet so well-protected, like nothing could hurt me, like I could feel no pain.

An angel? How is that even possible?

I don't get much time to linger on these thoughts before I feel Mikah squeeze a little tighter against my hip. "Wake up, sweetheart. We're here."

I blink my eyes a couple of times. I feel slightly energized. But I can still feel the worry and fear in my body, not because I'm afraid I'll be unwelcome or even that I'll overstay my welcome, but because of the emotions I feel for Mikah. I've given up everything I've earned for myself to come here.

He slowly pulls his arm away from me and I sit up. Feeling heavy and uncoordinated, like I'm just waking up, I rub my eyes and then look out the window. A man dressed in livery is coming through a revolving door and heading straight for the limo at a rather intense speed.

I freeze. I don't know who he is or why he's charging toward us.

Mikah notices my hesitation and is quick to explain. "That's Arthur. He's the building doorman."

I nod slowly as Arthur moves to the back of the limo where Andrew, I think, is opening the trunk for the bags.

Mikah slides past me to the door just as the red-haired gentleman opens it. Mikah climbs out. "Thank you, Connor." I smile a little at the name; it doesn't suit him at all.

As I start to get out of the limo, Mikah holds out his hand, almost automatically, and I use him to climb out. Standing next to Connor I feel like a child standing next to her dad. He has at least a foot and half on me, and he's taller even than Mikah.

Mikah leads me to the doors, but he bypasses the revolving door for the normal one. I can't help but smile at the idea that he's using it because of my claustrophobia. He really does pay attention. But I also notice that he doesn't let go of my hand as we walk through the door.

FOUR

Stepping inside the building, I see that the lobby décor is all tan and neutral tones with accents of black in the furniture. Opposite the door we've just come in is a security desk with a man sitting behind it.

"Good day, Mr. Blake."

"Hello, Charlie," Mikah replies to the man behind the counter. He's much older, heavyset with gray hair and glasses. He stands up in greeting as we pass toward the hallway to the right of the desk, and I find it comforting in some strange way to see a gun on his right hip.

We reach a bank of elevators but keep going, passing four different sets of doors until we come to the end of the hall. Directly in front of us is another set of elevator doors, and Mikah presses the up arrow. "This is the only elevator that will reach my apartment and where we're going."

As soon as he finishes, the bell chimes and I jump slightly. I know my fear is due to the fact that we're so exposed. Once we're in Mikah's apartment, I know I'll feel better.

As we step into the elevator, I see Connor and Arthur coming in through the front doors. Arthur has the duffle

28

bag. "Shouldn't we wait for them?" I ask, pointing in their direction.

"Nope, we're good to go up."

Mikah places a key card in a slot below the two buttons, then pushes the button for the sixth floor. I'd expected him to push the button for the seventh, assuming Mikah's apartment would be on the top floor.

"I thought we were going to your apartment?" I say, puzzled, as the elevator starts to climb.

He shakes his head and looks at me out of the corner of his eye. I can see a touch of worry in his expression. I remember he'd said something about my own apartment, but for some reason I thought he would take me to his. He's been so protective of me these last couple of days; I can't imagine him letting me out of his sight.

Before I can question him further about it, the elevator comes to a halt. The bell chimes again and I notice that, in a completely subconscious move, I inch closer to Mikah so that I'm standing behind his right arm, shielding myself.

The doors open on a hallway that is only a couple feet wider than the elevator doors. I can see straight down to a window at the far end.

Mikah takes a step toward the door, tugging me by my hand, bringing me with him. I slowly follow behind him. The hallway is drab: nothing on the walls, and the carpet has some crazy red and gold pattern on it. It makes me dizzy looking at it, so I look straight ahead as I follow behind Mikah.

We approach two doors, one on either side of the hall. "Red and his wife, Maria, live there." He nods toward the door on the left. "These are the only two apartments on this floor, and you can only access it by key card or a security code." I feel a little more comfortable now, knowing it's secure. "Also, Connor will be manning the hallway until around midnight, then Andrew will take over until morning."

He places a key in the door on the right, turns the knob, pushes it open and ushers me in. I look around cautiously and he reassures me, "Red checked it after we left the hospital. There is no one in here."

I take a few steps inside. The floors are a beautiful, light-colored hardwood. There is a closed door immediately to the right. "The laundry room," Mikah says, opening the door. Inside are a washer and dryer and some shelves with detergent and dryer sheets on them.

He steps across the hall. "Here is one of the bathrooms. The other is off of the main bedroom." He turns on the light. The tile is a pretty royal blue, the cabinets and accents a light wood.

What catches my eye, though, is the big, deep tub that has a step up in order to get into it. There are two faucets to fill it up. The idea of a warm bath is very inviting.

He pulls back, clicking off the light, and we proceed further into the apartment. It opens up to the right into the kitchen, which is bigger than my entire apartment. It's been done in beautiful dark countertops and cabinets, not quite black, that make the silver appliances stand out. A breakfast bar that separates the hall from the kitchen has three bar-height chairs whose color matches the cabinets.

He moves on, opening a door directly across from the kitchen. "Here's the second bedroom."

I peek inside: deep blue carpet; a white dresser and some matching bedside tables; light blue walls; and pictures of beaches, beach houses and even one of a pretty lighthouse.

"This room can be used for anything you want. Add a bed...or a crib." I can't begin to imagine what the softness in his voice on the last word means, but it's comforting.

I pull back from the door. "It looks lovely."

He smiles in return and closes the door again. He leads me into the living room and I'm surprised by how comfortable the space looks. There is an oversized L-shaped couch with large pillows and deep seats, the kind you just want to curl up on all day. On the wall in front of the couch is a large TV, probably the largest I've ever seen. Below that is an entertainment center that houses two sleek black boxes that are probably for the cable and maybe a DVD player.

The coffee table between the couch and the TV is made of wood similar to that of the floor, and underneath the table is a pretty, deep purple rug that stands out against the light furniture.

On the other side of the couch, the curtains pulled back, is a large sliding glass door leading out to a patio, and beyond that, a view that has captured my attention. The balcony overlooks the river down below, and I can see a barge making its trek upriver. Even with the trees nearly bare from the cold, the view is still breathtaking.

I sense Mikah's eyes on me, but I don't pay him much attention as I walk around the couch, wanting to have a better look at the view.

The door slides open easily, and a rush of air sweeps into the apartment – not overly powerful, but strong enough to cause my body to shiver. I step out onto the balcony and just stand there, dazed by the beauty below.

After a few moments, I feel my heart skip a beat and the hairs on the back of my neck stand up, then Mikah's hand on the small of my back.

"It's beautiful out here," I say, not wanting to pull my eyes away from the scene to look at him.

"This apartment has the best view. Come, I've got something else to show you."

I scowl at him. My heart pounds in my chest for reasons I don't quite understand, but I let him lead me back inside, his hand still resting on my lower back.

He reaches around and closes the door behind us. "Over here," he says, pointing toward a door on the wall opposite the TV I take a tentative step in that direction, unsure of why I'm hesitant now.

He reaches for the handle and pushes the door open.

FIVE

Beyond the door, the lights are on, low and warm. The room is decorated in purples: a purple comforter on the king-size bed, pillows in dark purples and lavenders, pale purple walls emitting the faint scent of new paint. Sitting in the middle of the pillows is a small bunch of what look like purple lilacs.

There are only three things in the room that aren't purple: two lamps and the carpet. On either side of the bed, two chrome lamps with cream-colored shades help to give the room its warm ambiance. The carpet is a light, not-quite-white shag that looks very plush.

I want to feel it between my toes. I kick off my skimpy ballet flats, sensing Mikah's delight as I step over the threshold and onto the carpet.

Realization dawns. "This room, this apartment...it's mine?" I ask quietly.

"Technically, I own it. However, it is yours for as long as you like."

Tears pool in my eyes as I take in what he's done. He knows that being on my own is important, but then he also knows that my living conditions were not great for me. Shame and gratitude wash over me in waves as I realize that Dr. Alston was right: no strings attached. If he wanted something in return, then I'd be in his apartment, but his giving me my own place proves even further that he really is only out to help me.

I feel him come up behind me. I turn quickly in his direction, throwing my arms around his waist.

"Whoa," he says, but I can hear his smile. "What's this for?"

I pull back slightly, unsure of what's come over me and afraid that I've overstepped some line, but his arms wrap around me, holding me to him, and I can no longer stop the silent tears from streaming down my cheeks.

"Thank you," I whisper.

His hand comes up to the back of my head. Gently, he strokes my hair, down my back, and for the first time, I feel a strong sense of comfort wash through me. I melt into his embrace.

The gravity of the last few days weighs heavily on my shoulders and my knees give out.

Mikah is quick to catch me as I let go. He reaches down and lifts me. I don't protest; the fight in me is gone. "Shhh, sweetheart, don't cry," he whispers, and I want to scream, to shout, to sob, to just break down. He reaches down for something I can't see, shifts slightly, and then he's pulling back the covers on the bed. He lays me down gently. I curl up into a ball, my back to him, and he slowly pulls the covers up to my chin.

He kisses the top of my head, then pulls back. I hear his jeans shift as he steps away, and his feet on the carpet, getting further away from me.

"Don't," I say through tears. "Don't leave."

I hear his sharp intake of breath. Then the door clicks closed. But the knob rattles as his hand comes away and he's walking toward me again.

I reach behind me and pull the covers back. He hesitates, and I turn my head to look at him. Worry and sadness mar his beautiful features. He's confused. I'm confused. I don't understand what is causing this need to have him close to me.

"Please," I say quietly, and his features thaw. Reaching down, he pulls the covers back a little further then climbs in, jeans and all. He turns so that he is closer to me, like last night. I roll back onto my side and his arm wraps around me. His other hand slides in under the soft feather pillow. He holds me close.

I tried to be strong. I tried to be everything I thought I needed to be for myself, and all that did was nearly get me killed. Again. Mikah was there to rescue me and nothing I can ever do in life will repay him for that. His generosity knows no bounds.

As he snuggles deeper into the bed, I realize that something is changing between us.

SIX

Walking. I'm still walking down the white hallway, though the opening seems to finally be getting closer. I'm suddenly reminded of what happened the last time, of the dark cave, the heat and screaming.

"Do not fear, you're safe."

Zirah?

"Yes?"

I don't understand.

"What don't you understand?"

Well, I'm here, in this hallway, walking toward something. Mikah, I believe.

"Yes, it is him. He's waiting for you."

But am I in the future?

"No, you are in the present day."

But how?

"You are in Elysium. You are in the land of your true self."

My hand slides along the baby bump - which is much larger than when I'm awake at home – letting the gesture silently ask my question of Zirah.

"It is because when you are in Elysium you are your true self. When you are on earth, you and your body

36

conform to normal standards so you don't alert anyone to the existence of the supernatural."

I'm confused by the fact that this doesn't all seem stranger to me. It all seems so natural, like second nature.

"That's because you've been here before, while you slept," Zirah says, answering a question I haven't asked. "When you were attacked, you were essentially dead, and that brought you into Elysium. While you were here, you learned of your fate." Her voice is reassuring.

Why don't I remember?

"You were not meant to remember. But it is why this all comes so easily to you. Mikah was primed by his mother - he was told of his legend in his younger years. You, Princess, were not." She pauses as if pondering something. "You were not meant to come to Elysium a few days ago."

Realization stumbles its way into my mind. *I died? He - Riley - he killed me?*

"Yes, but Mikah found you in time. He accelerated your healing and brought you back to Earth, which is where you are supposed to be. Your time has not come."

I mentally shake my head, trying to process all of this information.

"Dreams are a form of Elysium, Princess."

Princess?

"Yes, you are a princess of Elysium, and Mikah is your protector, your guardian."

I let that thought sink in deep. Mikah's my guardian. I was right: He really was only trying to help, to protect me.

I stop walking. *So my feelings for him aren't real?*

"Your feelings for your guardian are real, Vivienne. Never doubt them."

My heart leaps and I quicken my pace, anxious to be closer to him.

Finally he comes into full view. I watch him standing there, dumbfounded by what's happening to him. His wings are spread: full and beautiful in all their glory, white and perfect. My heart melts. Desire grows. I feel like a magnet being pulled toward something to attach to. Something to cling to.

He's looking at his arm now. The black tattoo that covers half of his body is detailed and beautiful. He is shirtless; my gaze lingers on his deeply defined biceps and his abs, which are on glorious display. His hips arc into a beautiful V that disappears into the waistline of his pants.

His skin is darker, seeming even more tan against the stark white of the room. I watch as he brings his hand up over his shoulder and takes hold of his wing. Instantly his eyes roll upwards, showing the whites, and his knees give way.

I giggle at his reaction and his head snaps up to look straight at me. I point to the mirror behind him. He cocks his head at me, so I point again, more urgently.

He turns slowly toward the mirror. I can see him squint and close his eyes. He takes a few steps in its direction and, after a beat, he slowly opens his eyes.

His eyes are a beautiful blue, like the ocean, warm with excitement. His spreads his arms wide; his wings are longer than his arm span.

I approach him quietly from behind. He stumbles slightly.

"Easy there, angel. You're alright."

He falters again but recovers quickly.

"What is happening to me?" His voice is strained, concerned, but there's a hint of wonder.

I watch as he slowly starts to move and flex his shoulders. His back is equally as toned as his front, and there is something extremely sexy about his wings. I giggle at how awkward he looks testing them for the first time, but his face lights up. He starts to turn toward me.

"No, no. Keep facing the mirror. Keep practicing," I say to distract him and watch as his expression changes to disappointment, but he continues to practice as I quietly sneak closer to him.

"Will I be able to fly?" I hear him ask as he watches the motions of his wings.

"Yes, in time." My answer surprises me – I didn't realize I knew that. Then I remember what Zirah told me. I try again in vain to recall being here before.

I'm within an arm's length of him. I reach out, tentatively, and lightly brush my fingertips along the feathers of his wings.

He moans – a sound born not of pain but of pleasure - and crumples to the floor. I touch him again, watching his eyes roll back and then close.

I smile at the idea that this is something he enjoys. I do it again and he moans once more.

I pull back slightly from him and begin to make my way around his now-collapsed wings.

"Keep your eyes closed," I breathe.

"But I need to see you." His voice confirms his need, but I have other plans before he opens his eyes.

I trail my finger along his nose to his lips, and he kisses the pad of my finger. My palm cups his cheek. He instantly leans into my touch. His skin is warm, slightly prickly from the stubble on his chin. My heart flutters at the excitement of touching Mikah.

"Give me your left hand," I say.

He slowly lifts his hand, and I recognize it as a calculated move, but it's unnecessary; I no longer feel threatened by Mikah.

As I take his hand, I kneel down in front of him. "Open your hand," I say.

He does so without hesitation, and I place it gently against my cheek.

A flood of emotion runs wild through my body. Tears form in my eyes and drip down my cheek. I can feel his tears, too. Something is shifting between us, a change in our relationship, a change that will bind us together.

SEVEN

There is a rather loud crashing sound behind me. I jolt and my eyes fly open. My heart is pounding, but I quickly realize that I'm back in the new apartment. I can hear some more shuffling behind me and I relax.

It's dark except for the light streaming through the slightly open door. Mikah is not in the bed with me.

I hear him curse.

I smile.

Then feel disappointed that I was pulled from the most bizarre and yet amazing dream I've ever had. If only it were true.

I sit up. There is a strange tingling sensation across my back and I scowl. It diminishes rapidly and I realize that I really need to pee.

I crawl out of bed, feeling slightly off balance as I stumble into the bathroom and close the door behind me.

I come out a couple minutes later, after running cool water over my face, realizing I would really like to take a bath, or at least a shower.

I quietly pad across the carpet to the slightly open door and peek through to see Mikah in the kitchen doing something near the stove. The air is filled with the smell of chicken and vegetables. Soup, perhaps?

"No, Seraphina," I hear him say, and my eyes scan the kitchen and the living room. There's no one that I can see.

Who's Seraphina? I wonder.

"She's his teacher," a familiar female voice says, and I spin around, stumbling into the chair next to the door in an ungraceful manner. Though the room is lit only by one soft light in the corner, I can clearly see that no one is in the room with me.

"Wha-?" I start to say.

"No need to talk aloud, Princess. I can hear you."

I shake my head. Princess? Wait, the dream.... I let the thought stop and I shiver.

"'Twas no dream. You are an angel, Vivienne, and a very special one at that."

How can this be happening?

"It is who you are, Vivienne, who you were always meant to be."

But if this is what I'm supposed to be, why then has all this... Words fail me as I let the reality of my dream sink in.

"Why have you had the life you've had? Well, your mother was once one of us, as well."

Once?

"She has fallen. She is one of our fallen angels. Though she has not sinned against the angels, she's chosen her own path."

She doesn't say any more, and I don't need any further explanation from her. My mother made her choice, her decision to be who she is. There is nothing I can do about that. She never showed any willingness to change her situation. She just kept on doing what she was doing. In a sense, I understand addiction and how it takes ahold of a person, but she never once expressed any need or desire to quit. Nor did she ever try on her own to quit.

Dread washes through me. I was never religious and have never gone to church, but I've read enough literature to know what heaven and hell are.

"Heaven and hell do not exist in that form, my child. When in your dreams you are in Elysium. Though very like heaven, it is far from it. Hell is a loose interpretation of what it is. Though Dante got it right."

Dante's Inferno*?*

"That's the one. Your mother, though fallen as she is, will not go to hell. She will still be among the souls in heaven, as you call it. Her choices and her actions were ruled by her substance abuse, and while she made all the wrong decisions in that life, she's never actually done anything to send her to hell."

But what about me? What about all the things she's done or let be done to me? Tears of frustration form. I understand what she's saying, truly I do, but what about the fact that she never so much as tried to protect me?

Realization dawns anew and I understand her words. I would never want to see my mother in hell. My mother is in a living, breathing hell of her own, lost inside her mind and trapped in a body that is riddled by her choices.

"Very well done, Vivienne. You're right - she suffers enough as it is right now. She does not need to suffer more. When she comes upon us, she will be free of her living prison, free of pain and suffering. Perhaps one day she will make amends with you."

Who are you? I ask inside my head, then fight the urge to go running and screaming from this room because I'm talking to someone or something inside my mind.

A soft laughter echoes around in my mind. "You are not crazy, dearest Vivienne. I am Zirah." The dream. "I am assigned to be your guide and your teacher, just like Seraphina is Mikah's."

Mikah's name brings me back to the present, to this room. *Does Mikah know about me?*

"He knows, more or less. The two of you have been having the same dreams; he is seeing the same as you are seeing in Elysium. However, he does not know that you're aware of being an angel when you're awake, and more than that, he does not yet see that the dream is shared and that you know he, too, is an angel."

I smile slightly at the idea that I know what he is, but he doesn't yet know that I know.

I smile wider as the memory of Mikah, asleep with his head on my bed when I woke up from the coma, comes to me. I knew instantly that his presence in the hospital was why I was alive. I knew that he'd saved me. The surge of devotion and gratitude I felt toward him in that moment was stronger than anything I've ever felt in my entire life.

Though I put up a fight about coming here to stay with him, I really didn't mean it. I knew the moment Riley came up behind me that Mikah was right all along: I'm no match for someone like Riley, someone who can easily overpower me. I needed help then, more than what Dr. Alston had been able to provide to me. I needed protection.

"He is your guardian, sweet Vivienne. What happens between the two of you now is up to the Fates. Go to him. Be with your angel," she says wistfully, and I feel a shimmer as she departs from my mind.

EIGHT

My stomach growls as the smell of warm chicken broth fills my nose. I get to my feet and turn toward the door. His back is to me still, but now he is at the breakfast bar with his laptop. I can't see what he's looking at, but the muscles in his neck are strained, tense.

I silently pull open the door and step onto the cool hardwood floor. As I pad quietly toward him, I see him stiffen, but he doesn't turn. The oddest of shimmers skates across his back, noticeable only because of the tight t-shirt he is wearing.

I say nothing as I come up to stand beside him, placing my hand on his back, right where I saw the shimmer. His breath rushes out of his lungs.

"Hi," I say as casually as I can manage, given that I know something he doesn't know.

"Hi," he says. His voice is raspy, slightly more so than normal, and the effect on my body is instantaneous. A shiver of anticipation zips across my back. "How did you sleep?"

I pull my hand away and place it on the of the bar stool.

"Wonderful, thank you. How about you?"

The corners of his lips turn up in a small smile. "Very well. Are you hungry?"

I nod, a little too enthusiastically, and he hastily closes the lid on his computer and stands.

"Good, the soup should be heated up. It's the same from the other day, is that okay?"

"Yes, that soup was delicious."

He busies himself in the kitchen, grabbing bowls, silverware and two placemats. As he puts them on the breakfast bar I take the seat in the middle.

"What would you like to drink?"

"Ice water is fine."

He scowls at me as he places the bowls and plates on the placemats.

"What?" I say. "I drink water all the time."

"How about some milk?"

I resist the urge to roll my eyes. "Fine," I say all breathy.

His lip twitches at my exasperated tone and he turns to the refrigerator.

When he opens it, I see that it is fully stocked with all manner of fruits and veggies, along with milk - which he takes out of the fridge - something that looks like iced tea, and a two-liter bottle of Mountain Dew. I smirk. He closes the door before I can inspect any further.

He grabs two glasses and pours us both some milk. I raise an eyebrow.

"What?" he says sheepishly.

I grin. "Never pictured you as a milk drinker."

He smiles. "I'm not, but if I'm forcing you to do it, I can do it, too."

I shake a little with silent laughter at his tone.

He reaches for three potholders sitting on the counter. Placing the biggest one between us, he takes the two smaller ones with him to the stove. He clicks it off, grabs both handles of the pot and brings the soup over to sit between us. Then he tosses the potholders aside and grabs a ladle as he comes around the bar.

In a very gentlemanly fashion he serves me first, then fills his own bowl.

When he's done, he takes the seat next to me. "How are you feeling?" he asks as I pick up my spoon.

I think about his question before answering. "I feel great, just really tired for some strange reason." I bring a spoonful of soup to my mouth, blow on it and take a sip. "Mmm," I moan, swallowing it down. "This is really good."

He too takes a bite and nods. We eat in silence for a little while. I drink down all of my milk and stand to get some more, but he stops me.

"I can get it," he says and stands quickly.

"I'm not broken, Mikah, I can do it." I try to sound sweet about it, but he scowls at me. I mentally shrug it off and go to the fridge for the milk.

"I never meant to imply you're broken."

My heart sinks a little bit as I realize it was more of an act of chivalry than waiting on me.

I return to my seat with the milk and begin eating some more. Before I know it, my bowl is empty and I still feel hungry. Just as I'm about to reach for the ladle, there is a knock on the door. I freeze.

"It's just Red," he says quietly as he takes in my frozen state. "He said he would be back with a change of clothes for me. I was hoping you wouldn't mind if I stayed on the couch tonight?" His gaze is warm, soft.

"Yes, please." I smile slightly. I hadn't thought about staying here alone, and Mikah's willingness to stay on the couch warms my heart, though I kind of wish he would sleep with me.

He walks toward the door. "I thought the couch would make you more comfortable," he says as he checks the peephole in the door. "Oh, it's Celeste." He reaches for the knob and then turns back to me, like he is seeking reassurance.

I nod hesitantly. I've at least met Red. Not sure if I trust him, but I've met him. Celeste is another story. I'd never realized I was so skittish about people before.

Then, as he opens the door, I'm reminded of the dream right before we left the hospital. Hearing Nyssa's name in that dream has given me the idea that people really aren't always as they seem. But I also don't yet know why she would be in my dream in the first place.

"Thank you," I hear Mikah say, pulling me from my thoughts.

"I'd love to meet her," a sweet, soft voice says from the doorway, and I watch as Mikah turns toward me.

I take a couple steps in his direction, and he opens the door a little wider.

"Come on in." He steps aside.

On the other side of the door is a very pretty yet average-looking woman with blond hair; big, blue eyes; and a warm, welcoming smile. She is taller than I am, though that's not hard to accomplish. I guess she's in her early thirties.

"Hi, Vivienne. I'm Celeste, Mr. Blake's housekeeper. It's a pleasure to finally meet you."

"Hi, Celeste. Your soup is fabulous," I say with a small smile.

"Thank you. I'm glad you like it. Can I get you guys anything else?" she asks, looking from me to Mikah and back again.

I shake my head.

"No, I think we're good for now," Mikah says to her, and she hands Mikah a bag.

"Vivienne, I'm not sure if you saw or not, but your closet has some clothing for you, mostly yoga pants and t-shirts. If something doesn't fit, let me know and I can exchange it for you."

I'm pretty sure my face shows the shock I'm feeling at the idea that there are clothes, not to mention that Mikah has spent money on me. "Th-thank you," I finally manage to mutter.

I see concern in Mikah's face as his brows knit together.

"You're welcome." She turns to Mikah. "Call if you need anything else. I'm going to take off for tonight, but I can come back if there's a need."

"Thanks, Celeste. See you tomorrow," Mikah says, and she waves at me. I wave back halfheartedly as she steps back out the door and Mikah closes it.

NINE

"Why did you buy me clothes?" I ask.

His back tenses and ripples at my words. The tension in his back is not anger; it's fear or worry.

"Mikah?"

I watch him come to a decision.

With his hands against the front door and his head down, he says quietly, "I wanted you to have a fresh start." He turns and leans against the door. His eyes are closed. "When you walked out of that hospital today, I wanted you to have a fresh start on everything. A new place to live, clothes on your back, proper food in the kitchen, and..." He pauses and opens his eyes. "I wanted to give you the tools you'd need to be able to take care of yourself." His voice is soft and his accent is thick.

I step back slowly toward the stool. I need to sit; my thoughts are swirling at a mile a minute. I can't speak. He's already given me so much. He saved my life. This just...it's too much.

"Vivienne, I needed to know that you'd be safe, that you'd stay safe, that I could give you the tools you needed to get back on your feet. Clothes, food, a job - whatever you need, it's yours."

I can barely hear him by the end of his speech. Eventually I get my mouth working again. "Why?" I breathe.

He runs his hands through his hair and pulls away from the door, slowly walking toward me. "Because..." He pauses in his stride, clearly deciding something. "Because you deserve it. There is no reason for you to live a life of poverty if I can easily prevent it."

"That's not what I asked. Do you do this for every girl in my situation?"

He shakes his head. His eyes are wary, unsure of my reaction. He should be unsure. He knows how much I don't want to be taken care of. Yes, I've progressed some in allowing him to bring me here, to give me shelter, food.... Are clothes really that much worse? I mean, I don't have any, and whatever clothes I had in my apartment should be burned.

He's wanting and willing to help me, and I push him away at every turn. Is it so terrible to let someone help me? No, it's not. But it's hard; I've fought for so long on my own that I don't know how to do this.

He watches me as I take in his words. The reality of what he's said sets in. Maybe he's right: Maybe I've been fighting for so long to prove that what my mother has put me through hasn't broken me. But for whom? Who am I trying to prove this to? I get fighting for myself, but for what else?

Am I trying to show my mother, prove something to her? For what? She's never been there for me. By doing it all on my own, was I just trying to prove that I don't need her, that I didn't need her? Or is it more than that? Am I really just being stubborn? It's hard to let go of everything I've done for myself, but what have I really accomplished? A shit job, a shit apartment, barely surviving.... How is that living?

I let out a deep sigh.

I wasn't living. I was alive, but not living.

I look at Mikah, whose face shows that he's worried about what I'm mulling over. The bottom line is this: I've obviously failed miserably at proving to myself that I can take care of myself. Maybe with a little help from him, I can get back on my feet, get back into a better place.

"Thank you," I finally manage to say, and his face and body instantly relax and a slow smile spreads across his lips.

"You're not mad?"

I shake my head slowly. "No, I'm not."

"Good. Okay." He's not sure what to say, as if I've taken away all his argument. "Are you still hungry?" I roll my eyes and he playfully scowls at me.

"Changing the subject much?" I tease him back.

He laughs. "Maybe a little." He looks at me expectantly.

"No, I'm alright for now."

"Good. I'll clean up the kitchen. What would you like to do?" His eyes follow mine toward the guest bedroom as I remember the huge, inviting bathtub in there. "Take a bath?" he asks.

I nod enthusiastically, and he turns on his heel.

"Why don't you go find some comfortable clothes, and I'll start your bath before I clean up."

I stand and head for the bedroom, hitting the light switch on my way in. I hesitate just a moment at the closet door, suddenly nervous about what I'm going to find in there. Then I realize that I've agreed to this, and I turn the handle at the same time I hit the light switch on the wall next to the door.

The closet is huge - about the size of the bathroom and equally as long - but thankfully it's not stocked full. Hanging up on the right-hand side are about ten different t-shirts, and below them are various pairs of pants, cotton ones by the looks of them. I also catch a glimpse of the dresser at the back of the closet, its top drawer slightly ajar.

I step up to it and pull open the drawer. Inside are several pairs of white and fun, colored socks and a stack of rather slinky looking underwear. I shiver at the idea of wearing what I'm looking at.

I pull open the next drawer: some bras and some other, not-so-slinky underwear. There are some really cute designer boy shorts and I start to feel excited; they look really comfortable.

I grab a bra and pair of underwear and turn back to the clothes. On the floor under the pants are two pairs of shoes: a pair of gray-and-white Converse and a pair of fuzzy slippers.

I smile and grab the house shoes, a pair of black pants and a t-shirt.

I leave the closet and head out into the living room to see Mikah in the kitchen cleaning up. "Did you find something?"

"I did, thank you."

He smiles at me and then nods in the direction of the guest room.

I scurry quickly through the bedroom toward the bathroom. The closer I get, the more pronounced the sound of the running water. I push back the door and I'm hit with a rush of steam that is warm and inviting.

TEN

Once inside the bathroom, I shed the purple scrubs - similar to the ones Amanda had given me last time - and drop Mikah's t-shirt to the floor with the pants.

For a moment I study my naked reflection in the mirror. It's almost as if nothing ever happened to me. Other than a faint, small line on the side of my neck and the brace on my wrist, there are no visible signs of my trauma.

I'm filled with satisfaction at the idea that I don't have to go through the nasty healing process. Was I really only out for a couple days?

Instantly, there is a shimmering sensation across my back, almost like a call to attention. I try to look over my shoulder but I can't see anything, so I turn so that my back is facing the mirror.

As my back becomes visible in the mirror, I do a double-take. A brilliant display of whites, blues, light purples and silvers form a beautiful wing-shaped tattoo across my back. My wings.

My head starts to swim as realization settles in, and I take a seat on the side of the tub.

The dream I could have written off as exactly that: a dream. The mental conversation with Zirah after I woke I could also have written off as some kind of momentary delusional episode. But this - these wings - solidify the reality of those dreams, the reality of my conversation, and the idea that my super-healing ability is a product of my true nature.

An angel? I muse as I fling my legs over the side of the ginormous tub. Reaching over to the faucet, I turn the water off.

The gentle swirl of jets under the water causes the surface to ripple slightly. There is a slight bubble film across the surface. I slowly sink down into the water, and my muscles begin to relax instantly as they're engulfed by the warmth.

I close my eyes and my mind drifts back to Elysium, but not like before. I'm not there; I'm just replaying the events from my dream this afternoon.

The emotions I felt about Mikah during that dream were heightened beyond anything I consciously feel for him now. The fact that my feelings for him in Elysium are so strong is intense and frightening, though I think a lot of that is due to my own self-preservation and holding back, to not wanting to admit to myself what Mikah really means to me.

He was genuinely concerned about my reaction to the clothes. He knew that I would be upset with him, and to be honest, I still am. But he's right: I can't work until at least after I see Dr. A. in a couple of weeks, and therefore I have no income and am incapable of taking care of myself. At least in the fashion that Mikah – and even maybe Dr. Alston - wants me to.

The bottom line in letting Mikah help me is that I have nowhere else to go. I'm essentially back to being homeless because I am unable to return to that apartment.

I also know, after Riley's attack, that I'm not able to protect myself.

Is Mikah capable of protecting me? I believe he is.

Suddenly my image of Elysium shifts to the image of the dark cave. I heard Nyssa's name. How does she fit into this? Where was I? In hell?

All these nasty unanswered questions. I can feel my anxiety growing quickly, but I'm brought out of my thoughts by a knock on the door.

"Viv, you alright?"

I smile. I'm in a tub for crying out loud. What could happen? "Yeah, I'm good."

"Holler if you need me."

"Okay." I can't help the smile that spreads wider. For some strange reason, I can still sense him on the other side of the door. I sink underwater, giggling as the idea of Mikah making sure that I'm okay and that I stay okay hits me. It's heady and mildly overwhelming, but at the same time it sends a ripple of happiness through me. Something similar to the way I felt in my dream.

ELEVEN

After what feels like forever, I finally climb out of the tub, warm and sleepy. After drying off, I put on the pants I pulled from the closet, noticing that they have a wide waistband that hugs my bump nicely. The pants are soft and comfortable. I forgo the bra, opting instead for just the t-shirt. Then I wrap my wet hair in a towel, grab my dirty clothes, and head out into the hallway.

I take a moment to really look around the apartment. Although it has rather expensive-looking electronics, it's also very common: no fancy artwork on the walls, no fancy leather furniture. It has a homey feel to it. Is this the way it's always been, or was it done this way just for me? I'm struck by a sudden curiosity to see Mikah's apartment.

Only then do I notice Mikah on the couch, his laptop on his knees and a look of intense concentration on his face. He doesn't notice me until I get closer. There are very few lights on in the condo, which is nice, and he's drawn the shades on the large glass patio doors.

The TV is on, but muted. I can't tell what's on, but it looks like news or sports.

Finally he looks up and smiles. "Feel better?" he asks.

I smile back. "I feel great. Just going to go put my clothes away, and then do you mind if I join you?"

"Not at all," he says as he closes his laptop and places it on the table in front of the couch.

I go dump my dirty clothes on the floor of the closet near the Converse, and as I come back out toward the living room, I see the TV flickering as he changes channels, looking for something to watch with me. His bare feet are stretched out on the coffee table.

I stand quietly in the doorway and just watch. So normal, so mundane. Not something I'd picture a big-time businessman doing on a Sunday night.

After a couple of minutes of watching him, I walk quietly around the couch to sit on the far corner opposite him.

"I don't bite," he says playfully.

I turn and smile at him. "I know."

"Then why are you sitting all the way over there?"

I shrug. "It seemed appropriate." All the other times we cuddled together have been on his initiative, and I don't feel comfortable pushing a boundary I'm not sure of.

He gestures with his outstretched arm for me to come closer to him.

A flash of excitement runs through me and I crawl across the couch toward him. I put my head on his shoulder and snuggle into him. It only takes a moment for him to bring his arm around me to rest his hand on my hip.

I let out a silent sigh of contentment.

"What would you like to watch?"

I shrug. "I don't care."

"Okay then."

He flips through a couple more channels and comes to settle on some show. My eyelids are very heavy so I'm not paying much attention. Before I know it, my eyes close and I'm asleep.

"Wake up, angel. Let's get you into bed." His voice is sweet. Wait, did he really just call me *angel*? "Come on, sleepyhead."

My eyes flutter just a little bit, but I don't want to move. I'm comfortable.

"Do you want me to carry you?"

I wiggle a little deeper into our cuddling. "No, just leave me here," I mumble.

He laughs. "Then where will I sleep?"

"Right here." I snuggle in a little deeper and hear his heart rate speed up. Unlike mine, it doesn't calm right away. But he continues to stroke my lower back, down near my hips, and I lean into his touch.

"See I knew you were awake. Come on, I'll carry you."

As he slides out from under my head and shoulder, I don't fight it but I don't help either, and I flop to the couch. I giggle a little bit and he reaches for my hand.

He pulls on my right arm and then is somehow lifting me. His other arm sweeps under my legs and just like that, he's carrying me. I don't put up a fuss, I just snuggle into his chest as he whisks me off to the bedroom.

TWELVE

The next morning I wake up rather early – five thirty, per the clock - and I fight hard for more than an hour to go back to sleep. When that fails, I climb out of bed.

I open the bedroom door quietly, remembering that Mikah's sleeping on the couch and hoping I won't wake him. But I find Celeste in the kitchen and Mikah sitting at the breakfast bar. He's working again on his laptop, papers spread out before him covering about half of the bar.

Celeste catches my movement and turns in my direction. She doesn't say anything, but she smiles at me and Mikah notices. He turns around on the stool so that he can see me.

"Good morning," I say quietly.

His smile lights up the room, prompting me to smile back at him.

"Good morning. Did you sleep well?" he asks as I start to walk toward him, running my hand through my hair as I do.

"I did, how about you?"

"I did. Didn't mean to wake you, though."

I shake my head. "You didn't. I've been awake off and on since about five thirty, but I wasn't ready to get up."

As I approach, he holds out his arms slightly in invitation. I take him up on it, and he wraps one arm around me, turning back toward the bar.

Movement on his computer screen catches my eye: I see a bunch of numbers ticking by across the top. I point. "What's that?"

He smirks. "That is the stock market."

"The what?"

Celeste lets out a chuckle as she goes back to whatever she was doing before. "Seriously, Mikah, don't bore her with the stock market. It's too early for that."

Mikah chuckles, and I can't help but smile at their exchange. "You're right," he says and closes the browser window.

I gasp. The background on his laptop is the same ultrasound picture that was in the frame he gave me.

"Sorry," he whispers. "I..." He doesn't continue.

"It's alright," I whisper back.

"I rather like that picture," he says as he looks at it again. "I hope it's okay?" His voice is quiet, shy.

I just nod, surprised. Not only did he take the picture in the first place, but he had it enlarged slightly for my frame and it's also on his laptop. I'm not sure how to process this new information.

Celeste interrupts my thoughts. "How about breakfast?"

Mikah looks to me. I look back at him, a little wary about the picture, but I'm rather hungry. I nod.

Mikah releases my waist and starts to gather up all of his papers. He reaches over to the middle stool and pulls it out. I walk around him and take a seat.

Within seconds of my sitting down, Celeste places a plate in front of me with an omelet that has diced-up ham and cheese sprinkled all over it. Next to it are hash browns. It smells amazing.

While I admire my food, she sets a plate of the same in front of Mikah.

"I'll be back a little later to clean up," she says as she leaves the apartment.

"Where is she going?" I ask, curious.

"To my apartment. She's not one to pry while others are eating," he says and smiles at me. "Eat up."

Picking up my fork, I dive in as my stomach begins to rumble.

Once we've finished eating, Mikah is quick to clear the bar of our dishes, placing them near the sink.

"Would you...would you like some hot chocolate?" he asks.

I give him an amused look. "You drink hot chocolate?"

He turns to me, smiling. "No, I drink coffee, but I wasn't sure if you'd like it."

"I'd love some hot chocolate."

He turns and reaches for a cupboard door. Inside are all manner of plates, bowls, glasses, wine glasses, and mugs. He grabs two mugs and then reaches for the kettle on the stove. Sliding to the left of the stove, he opens another cupboard; I can't actually make out its contents because he grabs something and closes it quickly.

He goes back to where he left the mugs. I can't see from this angle what he's doing, but watching him move about the kitchen, making me hot chocolate, has me thinking about how thoughtful and caring he is.

A couple moments later I hear the clinking of silverware against ceramic, then the noise stops and he turns around with a mug in each hand.

"Here you go." He sets them down on the bar.

I smile as I pick up the purple and blue mug. It's comfortably warm to the touch, and I can see little billows of steam rising.

He turns to put the stirring spoon in the sink. "Would you..." As I blow across the top of my hot chocolate, he takes a deep breath and starts again. "Would you like to see my apartment?" he asks with his back toward me. I see the tension in his back and shoulders and can feel it in the air.

"Of course," I say, and he relaxes. I'm not sure why he is so worried about me seeing his apartment. "I'd love to." I put the mug down without taking a sip, push back from the bar and stand up. I feel a little dizzy, but I recover quickly. "I'll go change," I say.

"No need, just grab your slippers. It's right upstairs," he says, finally turning to look at me. His eyes are bright and he's excited. So why the tension?

"Alright, I'll be right back."

I move quickly toward the bedroom, a little excited to see his apartment. Curious to see what Mr. Suit lives in. I have no doubt that this apartment was furnished with me in mind. All the furniture here is soft and comfortable, normal and everyday. Is his apartment like this too?

I grab my slippers from the closet and step into them, then turn off the bedside light before heading back into the living room.

As I come back out of the bedroom with my slippers, he hands me my mug. "You can bring that with us. Are you ready?"

I nod as I blow across the top of the mug and finally take a sip. It's really good.

"Come on, sweetheart," he says, and I follow him to the door.

I smile at the term *sweetheart*, something so simple yet so powerful at the same time. He's called me sweetheart before, but somehow, here in this apartment, it means more.

THIRTEEN

Connor is standing on the other side of the door when Mikah opens it. "Good morning, sir," he says quickly.

"Good morning, Connor. We're just going up to my apartment."

Connor nods quickly and steps aside.

Mikah and I head down the hall and Connor, thankfully, doesn't follow.

When we reach the elevator, Mikah slides a card in a reader over the arrows and presses up. "I'll give you this card. In order to come upstairs, you need to swipe it, then press the up arrow. You're welcome upstairs anytime you want," he says as the elevator chimes and the doors open.

Once again I notice that I'm standing slightly behind Mikah as we step inside the elevator.

Mikah pushes the button for the seventh floor and the doors close. He switches his mug from his right hand to his left, then slowly brings his arm down to his side. His fingers brush against the back of my hand. I turn it slightly, opening it to him, and he takes it into his. A charge develops between us and I can't stop myself from smiling.

The elevator chimes again and the doors open on a small entryway, about ten by ten feet. Andrew is standing in front of the only door.

"Good morning, sir," Andrew says. He directs a friendly smile at me. "Good morning, ma'am," he says sweetly, and I know I blush crimson.

"Good morning," I say back shyly as Mikah lets go of my hand and reaches for the door.

We step into a small hallway and Mikah releases my hand to close the door behind us.

"Does he always stand there?"

Mikah grins. "No. I'd mentioned to Celeste before you woke up that I might bring you up here. She obviously told them, and they made adjustments. Security on my floor is tighter than on yours. You really can only access this floor by keycard, the pass code does not work." He's looking at me with a reassuring look on his face. "There are cameras throughout this building. Anytime seven is pressed, it activates an alarm in Red's apartment, one on his phone, and a video feed showing who is in the elevator. He also has a control to stop the elevator if someone who should not be here managed to gain access."

Holy crap, it's like a fortress in here. Suddenly I feel safer than I've ever felt in my entire life. I know my eyes are wide and Mikah can sense my immediate mood change.

"I will let nothing happen to you," he says then smiles. "Come on, let's have a look, shall we?"

I nod and he takes my hand again.

The hallway is similar to mine, only shorter and with only one door on the left-hand side. We reach it, and Mikah opens it up.

We go through the door into a living room that has plush gray carpeting, a coffee table, an L-shaped couch similar to the one downstairs, and a massive TV surrounded by speakers. Shelves beneath the TV hold a ton of movies. The lone door on the opposite wall is closed. I turn around to find that the door we've just come through is flanked by two massive bookshelves stacked full of books.

"Do you like to read?" Mikah asks me softly.

"I love to read," I reply and walk toward the shelves. When you do anything you can to avoid being at home, sometimes the library is the only place you can go. The books are arranged in alphabetical order by author and range in type from thrillers to romance to classic literature. "You have good taste," I say as I pull out Louisa May Alcott's *Little Women*.

I hear him snicker. "I suppose. I have several books, including that one, that were my mother's."

I gently place the book back on the shelf.

"You're more than welcome to help yourself to anything you see here. If there is something you'd like to read that isn't here, let me or Celeste know and we will get it for you."

I look over my shoulder at him. "There are more books here than I could ever imagine in one private library. I'm sure I can keep myself entertained with this lot."

As I turn to face him, he heads toward the door on the opposite wall and opens it to reveal a hallway. I go through, and he follows close behind.

The floor here is hardwood, and this hallway is longer than the one on the other side. An open door directly in front of me reveals a toilet and sink. Then I notice a closed door to my left.

Zoey Derrick

"That leads to the stairwell and is often what Red uses to come upstairs," Mikah says.

He leads me toward the right. We pass by a couple of closet doors along the left wall, and then the hallway opens up into a rather large space. The wall in front of me from here to the end of the room is made entirely of glass, and on the other side is a large patio with the same view of the river as I have from my patio downstairs. At various points all along the glass wall there are doors that lead out onto the patio.

The room itself is cavernous, with ceilings at least two floors high. The floor is a beautiful light hardwood that stands out against the dark furniture. Between us and the patio is a large dining room table set for eight, and at the far end of the room to the left is a sitting area, with tall chairs in a loose circle formation around a coffee table. To the right is the kitchen, done in the same cupboards and countertops as my apartment: dark wood cabinets and black countertops with stainless steel appliances. I put my mug on the counter.

Behind me I hear a door click open. I turn toward Mikah, who has been silent while I've been looking around his apartment.

"And this is my bedroom," he says, and again I see the tension in his features.

He flips on a light. I cross over to him and take a step into the room, and my heart stops.

FOURTEEN

I can't focus on anything besides the king size, four-poster bed that dominates the room. It's *the* bed, the one from the dream I had the other night at the hospital. The one where...

I let the thought end there as the image of Mikah and me, cuddled inside this very same bed with its tall canopy and stacked block posts, fills my mind.

I look to Mikah, who is still tense. Was he in that dream, too? Did he see us as I saw us?

"It's beautiful," I breathe, and he relaxes. I'm not sure whether he's tense because he is showing me his room or whether it has something to do with that dream.

"The closet and bathroom are to your left," he says, and something is different in his voice. It's almost husky.

I look in that direction and see a large opening into a closet area. His clothes are hung neatly, shirts across the top bar and pants and jackets along the bottom bar. But I don't stare too long; closets and bathrooms are personal space.

I look back to the bed once again and wonder: Will that be me? Us? Someday, one day soon? I remember from the dream that I was much larger than I am now, nearing the end of my pregnancy. But Mikah in the dream was just as sweet then as he is today. Tender in a very un-masculine way.

Mikah takes me through the rest of the house, leading the way back across the main room into a guest bedroom on the other side of the house and then his office.

As we come out of the office back into the main room, he comes to a sudden stop. "Hello, Red."

I peek around the doorjamb. Red is standing near the breakfast bar.

"Hello, sir. Vivienne," he says and nods in my direction.

"Hello," I say quietly.

He smiles and turns back toward Mikah. "Chrys is here. Shall I have Andrew bring him up?"

Mikah looks quickly to me then back to Red. I can feel my brow furrow.

"Give me about five minutes, then go ahead and bring him up," Mikah says to Red, but he is still looking at me.

"Yes, sir," Red says and walks toward the entryway.

"Who's Chrys?" I ask as soon as Red is out of sight.

Mikah takes a couple of steps into the sitting area in front of his office.

"Chrys is my lawyer. The one I'd like you to talk to about..."

"Do I have to?" I ask.

"No, you don't. But Stevens will be here around one. I'd like you to have some time to discuss things with Chrys before Stevens arrives. I'd like Chrys to be present while Stevens is here."

"I don't understand why all this is necessary." I lean into the jamb of the office door and take a long, deep breath.

"I'm not entirely sure it's necessary either. You've done nothing wrong, but I...I'd like Chrys to be here as a buffer from Stevens. He'll know if the questions are crossing the line or making you uncomfortable. And..." He pauses. "And he can help keep me in line from doing or saying something I shouldn't to Stevens." He runs a hand through his hair.

"I don't mind talking to Chrys as much as I mind talking to Stevens. The only thing that I have to tell him, he already knows." My voice is soft but I'm suddenly very nervous. "Or he should know. He would have access to my medical file as far as my injuries were concerned. If he suspects anyone other than that asshole, then he's barking up the wrong tree."

Mikah nods. "I know, sweetheart. I don't know what it is that he's after, what information he thinks you can provide that he doesn't already have. But unless there is some legal way out of you talking to him, I can't hold Stevens off forever, as much as I'd like to." I can see the concern in his eyes.

"I'll talk to both of them if it means that once it's done, it's done, and I don't have to do it again."

I have a gut feeling that it's a waste of time to talk to either one of them. If that cave dream is any indication, I have a feeling that whoever that dark voice belongs to is having his own way with Riley. I shudder.

After a few heartbeats of silence, I hear a door close and shoes clicking across the hardwood floor. I lean back, shrinking into his office as a rather tall, well-dressed man emerges from the hallway.

FIFTEEN

For being a lawyer, Chrys is surprisingly gentle when it comes to asking me questions. It's hard to talk about again, and I can tell Mikah is uncomfortable with my answers, but they're the same ones I gave him in the hospital on Saturday night. I'd hoped that Mikah could act as a buffer and handle most of the answers, but Chrys is adamant that the answers come from me and me alone.

When I'm finished telling Chrys everything I remember, I say, "I don't want to talk to Stevens."

"I don't see any reason for you to talk to him," Chrys replies matter-of-factly. "The evidence of what happened to you is in your medical file. You can identify Riley in a lineup if necessary."

I shudder at the idea of having to look at him again.

Chrys continues, "With the previous case, Riley presents with a history of violence toward you, the police shouldn't need anything more. I will try talking to Stevens first, see what it is that he's after, and then we can go from there." He doesn't look at Mikah when he talks, which is reassuring.

Chrys is rather handsome, with dirty blond hair that falls to just below his ears. Definitely doesn't seem like the lawyer type. Maybe that's why I can talk to him without issue. I've never had to deal with a lawyer before, and if I ever have to deal with one again, someone like Chrys would be great. He's not abrasive in any way, and I like that.

"I have a feeling he just wants to see her, talk to her, maybe even apologize to her," Mikah says, and I look at him, puzzled. "He's pretty messed up over what happened to you, and while I'd like to wring his neck for letting it happen, in the end he and his department were hurt far more than you were."

I nod slowly, taking in his words. I remember him telling me about the cop who was parked outside of my apartment and how he was killed. Guilt knots my stomach. If Stevens hadn't felt it necessary to protect me from Riley, his cop would still be alive. In a way, it's my fault that the officer died.

"I'll talk to Stevens," I blurt out. "Despite the fact that what happened to me happened, he deserves a chance to say his piece."

Mikah looks at me, awe etched on his features.

"Okay, would you like me to talk to him first?" Chrys pulls my attention away from Mikah.

I nod. "Sounds good to me."

I hear the door open and the squeak of tennis shoes across the floor. "Lunch is ready downstairs," Celeste says.

"Chrys, would you like to join us?" Mikah asks him.

"No, I'm going to make some notes. I'll take a sandwich, though, if you don't mind."

Mikah turns to Celeste. "Would you mind?"

"No, not at all," she replies and walks into the kitchen.

"Chrys, why don't you call me when Stevens is ready. I'll tell Red to bring him up here and you can chat with him first. We will come back up when it's time." Mikah stands and offers me his hand. I take it and stand too.

"Sounds good," Chrys replies, and Mikah and I head for the door.

SIXTEEN

We've barely finished our lunch of salad and chicken soup - I'm thankful this soup is so good, otherwise I might tire of it - when Mikah's phone rings.

"Blake," he answers. I see his face fall slightly.

We haven't talked too much over our meal. I get the impression that Mikah is waiting for me to talk. Though about what, I'm not sure. Or maybe he is just trying to make sure that I really am okay after what's happened to me.

"Alright, Chrys, we'll be up in a moment," I hear him say, then he shifts the phone and pushes a button.

"Chrys says that Stevens is satisfied with what he's told him regarding what happened," Mikah says rather stoically, as if he's thinking about something.

"I'm still mad at him," I say quietly. I look up at him and he smiles.

"That makes two of us." Mikah wraps his arm around my shoulder and pulls me close. He lightly kisses the top of my head. "It will be okay." He squeezes my shoulders. "How are you feeling?" he asks.

"Okay. Just tired."

"Alright, we'll make this quick and you can come down here and take a nap."

"Will you join me?"

He smiles a little wider. "Maybe." He grins.

I smile back and we head for the door and back upstairs.

As we walk into the apartment, I hear Chrys talking but I can't really make out what he's saying. We come around the corner to find Stevens, Chrys and another cop - one of the ones from Thursday night, whose name I can't remember - sitting at the dining room table.

Stevens stands and turns to face us. Mikah still has his arm around me protectively, but Stevens smiles when he sees me.

"Hi, Vivienne," Stevens says, then he points in the direction of the other cop, who's now standing as well. "This is Officer Ruiz."

"Hi," I quietly, not sure why I'm so shy.

Mikah leads me a little closer to the table and Stevens comes over. He's dressed in full uniform, though I notice that both his and Ruiz's gun holsters are empty. Red must have made them leave them downstairs.

"How are you feeling?" Stevens asks. There is a lot of emotion playing on his features.

"I'm okay, just very tired."

"I'm sorry, Vivienne. Very sorry," Stevens says. His voice breaks and I can see raw emotion in his eyes. The look makes my heart lurch.

"Stop. I'm alive, it's alright," I say, and as I do, I realize that it really is okay. I have no reason to be mad at Stevens or anyone else for what happened to me, except Riley. "Riley is a very driven individual. He will let nothing stand in the way to getting what he wants," I say, and Stevens relaxes a little bit. I step out of Mikah's arm and gently hug Stevens. I feel all eyes on me as I do this, but I understand the pain he is going through. If it helps him heal from what happened to me, I'll do it again and again.

"You're too kind to me, Vivienne." He wraps his arms gently around me and squeezes just a bit. I can tell he's being cautious.

I pull back. "Is that the only reason you're here?" I ask and step back.

Mikah is quick to wrap his arm around me, and exhaustion washes over me.

"No, I wanted to ask you a few questions, but Chrys has answered most of them for you."

Mikah leads me to the table and pulls out a chair for me.

"Thank you," I say as I take a seat.

Stevens, Chrys and Mikah all sit. Ruiz stays standing about ten feet away.

"I just wanted to ask you a couple of follow-up questions. I'll make this quick, promise," Stevens says. "First, Mr. Crowley, downstairs from your apartment. Do you know whether he would have let Riley into the building?"

The mention of Mr. Crowley brings a knot to my stomach. "I don't think so. He knew his tenants pretty well. Especially if Riley said my name, he wouldn't have let him in."

"That's something we've been trying to figure out, how he got into the building."

"Again, Riley's determination got him into that building. I vaguely remember Mr. Crowley's door being open when I got home. I didn't think much of it because he's done it in the past when he's run off to a tenant's apartment," I say, my voice still quiet and weak. But Stevens is listening intently.

"Detective, do you know why his door was open?" Mikah asks.

Stevens face scrunches up a bit. "Mr. Crowley was..." He pauses and looks at me. I nod slightly for him to continue. "He was killed. From what we can tell, it happened before he got to you."

I feel my eyes fill with tears. Mr. Crowley was a really nice man. He didn't deserve this.

"How do you know that?" Mikah asks.

Stevens shifts uncomfortably in his chair. "We, uh..." He looks to Officer Ruiz then back down at the table. "Forensics came back on Vivienne's apartment. We found a t-shirt that wasn't Vivienne's. It was white, and it had several spatters of blood on it. We found three types of blood." I flinch. "Vivienne's, Mr. Crowley's, and what we can only assume is Riley's, as it doesn't match any DNA in our system, but it matches DNA on a couple of hair fibers we found in Mr. Crowley's apartment as well as-" He pauses again, looking at me. "-on Rebecca."

I can feel the tears sliding down my cheeks. "That asshole," I spat. "I get it, I get me, I get why me, but damn it why them?" The tears are flowing harder. I bury my head in my hands and start to sob.

I vaguely hear Chrys. "I think we're done here. If you have any more questions for her, contact me. Or when you capture him and need an identification, let me know."

"Come 'ere, Viv." I feel Mikah's hand across my shoulders. His other hand snakes under my legs as he pushes the chair back and picks me up. "Here or downstairs?" he whispers.

"He-" I can't finish, but he catches my words and he turns toward his room.

SEVENTEEN

For two weeks Mikah barely steps foot out of the building, staying with me no matter what comes up. We talk, watch movies and take naps, and when he needs to do some work-related things, I indulge in his library. About a week into our self-imposed seclusion, I finally start to feel more like myself. I have a little trouble with being tired, but sometimes I think it is because I'm not doing much. Mikah and I start taking morning walks along the river, when the weather is decent.

Connor, Andrew and Red are ever-present in and around the two apartments, and I take it upon myself to get to know Connor and Andrew a little. They are really nice guys, and I get the distinct impression that they are naturally protective.

Zirah hasn't made an appearance since the Sunday I was released from the hospital, though, strangely, I keep having the same recurring dream about the white hallway and Mikah. I always seem to wake up right before we kiss, and it is getting to the point of frustration. I want to know what's going to happen next.

Mikah and I grow close, but he hasn't so much as kissed me - well at least on the lips - and it's starting to feel like my dream: so close and yet so far away.

Then he has some pressing business to deal with in Phoenix, and he leaves me alone for the first time since bringing me here.

I miss him like crazy, and it doesn't quite feel like home without him here. The house is far too quiet; I leave the iPod he gave me - loaded with music and hooked up to the stereo system – on all the time. When he first gave it to me, of course, I rebuffed the gift, telling him it was too much and there was no need to spend his hard-earned money on me. He wouldn't hear it. Eventually I relented and kept it.

I'm in my bedroom, getting dressed for my appointment with Dr. Alston, when I realize for the first time that my breasts seem very swollen and tender. I was never well-endowed in that department, but holy crap, these things are getting huge. My nipples are puffy and turning a dark, almost cherry wood color.

I turn around to look in the full-length mirror on the back of the closet door. I'm a little shocked by what I see.

My eyes are a bright blue, bluer than I've ever seen them before. I turn completely sideways and look toward the mirror. Of course I've noticed my belly getting bigger physically, but I've never really looked at it like this. Okay, it's not huge, but it is definitely there, and it looks....

Tears prick at my eyes. Good tears, but damn. This whole thing is really sneaking up on me.

I face the mirror head on again, and now I can see why I really hadn't noticed it much; from this angle it looks cute and tiny, small compared to my breasts.

I notice too that my hips are softer, the bones no longer as defined as they once were. All the food I've been eating, plus the vitamins that Mikah has been making me take three times a day, have no doubt been helping me put on some weight. But it appears to be really good weight.

My face has completely filled in, rounded, and there is a flush to my cheeks, no doubt because I've been looking at myself in the mirror. My collarbones are still visible, but in a very healthy, almost sexy way.

"Sexy?" I say. I've never thought of myself as sexy before.

A knock on the bedroom door causes me to jump, like I've been caught doing something I'm not supposed to do. I cover myself instinctively as Andrew's accented voice comes through the door. "Vivienne, we have about five minutes before we need to leave."

"I'll be right there," I holler back and slip the bra on. It's a little bit snug in the chest and made from a thin, sheer material. My nipples poke through like nobody's business.

Standing here in my sheer black bra and black yoga pants, I cannot help but admire myself. For once in my life I actually look and feel pretty. I flush at the thought and reach for a black tank top, then I grab an old Boston College hoodie I inadvertently "borrowed" from Mikah a couple of days ago. It's soft, huge, and warm. I throw it on and head out the bedroom door.

EIGHTEEN

Within a matter of moments we're out of the apartment, down the elevator and into the lobby. Connor is standing next to a sleek black SUV, something I've never seen before. The windows are tinted really dark, and it looks mildly intimidating. Andrew opens the rear passenger door for me just as Connor slides in behind the wheel. I clamber in, noticing that the window on the driver's side is down, wiping out my anxiety of tight spaces. Andrew shuts the door behind me. He is quick to slide into the front passenger seat, and we're off.

I take a deep breath. "What's the big rush?" I ask.

Connor peers at me through the rearview mirror. "Safety precaution, ma'am."

I roll my eyes, whether at the safety comment or the fact that he called me "ma'am," I'm not sure. "Call me Vivienne, please, Connor?"

"Yes, ma'am."

I scowl at him.

"Vivienne," he corrects himself.

"Thanks."

He turns back to the road, driving at a speed I'm not entirely sure is legal. I watch out the window as we make our way through downtown. It is Friday morning and the traffic is moving quickly.

A few minutes later we pull into the parking garage at H.C.M.C. Connor steers the car up the ramp to the third floor of the structure and pulls up at a door.

Andrew climbs out of the car, moving a little slower now. Is that deliberate?

He opens my door and I climb out. I expect Connor to drive away to a parking space as soon as Andrew shuts the door behind me, but the SUV doesn't move. Andrew walks with me through the automatic doors into the hospital.

"Do you know where we're going?" I ask Andrew.

"I do." He looks down at me with his bright blue eyes, and his thin lips stretch into a friendly, reassuring smile.

I smile back. Andrew has been really nice to me these last couple of weeks.

We round a corner, and it's practically a dead end except for a door to the right. Andrew goes straight to it and knocks.

"Come in," I hear a woman on the other side of the door say.

Andrew opens the door. "Hi, Dr. Alston," he says. "Vivienne is here to see you."

"Of course. Come on in."

Andrew steps in and stands with his back to the door, holding it open for me. I sneak in between him and the jamb to see Dr. Alston sitting behind a desk.

"Is there any other way into your office?" Andrew asks.

"No, just the room behind you, but no outside access," she says, looking at the same door Andrew is leaning against.

Andrew quickly figures it out and checks the other room. Then, turning back to me, he says, "I'll be right outside if you need me."

"Thanks," I say, and he slips out, closing the door behind him.

"Hello, Vivienne, how are you doing?" she asks as she looks me up and down.

"Great," I say, but I feel a little uncomfortable at her gawking.

"You look amazing," she says with a bright smile on her face, and I relax. "You've put on some weight. Good job."

I blush a little bit. "It's all the food Mikah's been feeding me."

She laughs. "I'll bet. Come in, have a seat."

"Thanks." I do as she says and take a seat in the chair across from her. Then I look around her office. It's decorated in warm browns and tans, not sterile at all, but rather homey looking. She has a few landscape pictures on her walls, but nothing clinical. Though there are no windows, the room is well lit by lamps. The florescent lights overhead are off.

"So, you've been eating okay?"

"Yeah. I have some issues with meat, particularly red meat. The smell turns my stomach," I say, making a face.

"That's not all that uncommon. When we're pregnant, our bodies tend to crave the things it thinks it needs and reject the things it doesn't, or at least doesn't like. What about white meat? Like chicken or pork?"

I notice that as she asks these questions she isn't very doctorly – if there is such a word. She's talking to me like I'm a person, not a patient, and I warm up to her a little bit more.

85

"If I don't smell it in raw form, I'm okay, though mixing it into pastas or soups makes it easier for me to eat," I tell her.

"What about vitamins, have you been taking them?"

I nod. "Three times a day." Partly because Mikah is insistent about them, but I leave that part out. "The one in the morning makes me a little nauseous, but it doesn't last for very long."

Her cell phone rings. I don't expect her to answer it, but she picks it up. "Dr. Alston." She listens for a moment. "Hi, Mikah." Oh, fabulous. He's checking up on me. "I don't see why that would be a problem, but have you asked Vivienne?" She pauses again. "Well, she's right here. Want to ask her yourself? Alright, hang on."

NINETEEN

She reaches across her desk to hand me her phone. "It's Mikah," she mouths.

I take the phone from her, shaking my head in disbelief. "Hello."

"Hi, sweetheart. Look, I wanted to be there but I can't. I'm still in Phoenix taking care of stuff, but I'm wondering if it would be alright if I video conference in on your appointment?"

What? "Why?"

There is a pause on the other end of the line. I'm about to say *hello* again when he pipes up. "I really wanted to be there to support you today, and I can't, so...well...I was hoping this would be okay."

I take a deep breath - not in anger or frustration, but at the fact that this is one of the many signs he's shown over the last couple of weeks that there is more than friendship between us. His persistence in making sure I'm well taken care of extends to the baby, and I don't want to deny him this.

"It's fine, though I have no idea how-"

"Don't worry about it, Dr. Alston knows. Hand the phone back to her and I'll see you in a minute."

"Ohhkaaay." I hand the phone back to Dr. Alston, my stomach flip flopping with excitement at the idea of seeing Mikah. Sure, I'd talked to him on the phone last night, but it's not the same. Speaking of which: Why didn't he bring this up last night?

"Sure, okay. Call me back in about ten minutes and we should be ready." She pulls the phone away from her ear and presses a button. "Are you sure you're okay with this?"

"Yeah, it just took me by surprise. I talked to him last night and he didn't mention anything about wanting to be here."

She shrugs. "I'll set him up so that he can't see much more than a little bit of you and the monitor. I'd like to do another ultrasound, just to check on progress. After today, we will wait a couple of months for another one."

I nod, a little excited at the prospect of seeing my baby again.

"Did you open the envelope I gave you last time?"

"Envelope? What..." I think back for a moment. "Oh, you mean the one where you wrote down the baby's sex?"

She nods and smiles wide, hopeful.

"Um, no," I say shyly.

"Do you really not want to know?"

I think about it for a minute. What are the reasons to not know? Other than the surprise when it's born? "I guess I kinda forgot about the envelope. I haven't seen it since you gave it to me. But yes." I smile wide. "Yes, I want to know."

Dr. A., in a very uncharacteristic manner, starts clapping excitedly. I can't help but laugh at her reaction.

"Come on, let's have a look." She stands, comes around her desk, heads toward a door next to the main door into her office and opens it.

I stand hesitantly, not sure where she's taking me.

"I have a private ultrasound and exam room in here."

Oh.

I follow her into the room. This room is a little bit more clinical, but it's still decorated in the light tans with red as an accent color, and it looks nice. There are a couple of monitors near the head of a short bed that has stirrups coming off of the end.

"I'm going to step back into my office. I would like you to remove your pants and underwear." She hands me a blanket, similar to the one that was on my hospital bed. It is far from warm, but it beats sitting here naked. "Climb up and cover yourself with this when you're done. Once we're done with Mikah and the ultrasound, I'd like to do an internal examination, if that's alright."

I nod and she turns to leave.

TWENTY

After just a minute or so I hear her knock. "You all set?" she asks through the door.

"Yeah," I call back, and she comes in.

"Go ahead and lie back," she says as the thing in her hand starts ringing. It's not a phone; it's similar, but bigger, white with the Apple logo on the underside. She pushes a button and waits. "Hi, Mikah," she says and then turns the machine toward me.

"Hi, beautiful," he says to me, and I can see his smile, big and bright.

"Hi," I say, blushing at his words.

"Mikah, Vivienne has decided that she wants to know the sex of her baby. Do you want to know, too?" Dr. A. asks.

Mikah's face lights up. "If she wants to know, then I'd like to know, too." The whole time he says this, it's as though his eyes are boring into me, searching, seeking, wanting. Similar to the way he looked at me when I first met him at the diner.

"Okay then," Dr. A. says. She walks around to the other side of the bed from the ultrasound machine and places the device into a holder of some sort that is attached to the bed. "How's the view, Mikah?"

I now notice the little image in the corner of the screen that shows what Mikah can see. It isn't much, really: a little bit of my bump, but more of the machine that Dr. Alston is now standing at. She turns the monitor toward us. "This might be a little shaky on your end, Mikah."

"Alright. Viv, you okay?"

"Yeah," I say to Mikah.

Dr. A. proceeds to push my sweatshirt and tank top up so that my belly is exposed. Once that's done, she goes for the bottle and squirts nice, warm gel along the lower half of my belly. Then she brings out the small, flat-headed wand and gently presses it to my stomach.

Everything is very quiet as Dr. Alston does her thing with pushing buttons.

I can see the baby's heart pumping wildly. She pushes another button and the echoing sound of a heartbeat fills the room.

She moves the wand around a little more and the head comes into focus. It looks similar to last time, but this time it's bigger; there isn't as much black surrounding the baby as the first time.

She points to the monitor. "There are the eyes, nose, lips and chin. See this string of pearls? That's the baby's spine." I watch as the baby moves. "Oh, I see. A little showoff." She laughs and moves the wand again. "There's an arm, and the other one is...right there." She moves her finger up on the screen, pointing at a faint, translucent white line in the background, leading up to a cluster of shorter white lines. "The other hand."

She moves her hand down further on the screen at the same time she moves the wand. "A leg," she says.

I'm starting to be able to see what she's pointing out. She moves the wand again to my right side, and I can see feet. Two of them with little tiny bones. As if on cue, the baby spreads its legs, and one foot goes off the screen.

Dr. Alston laughs. "Yup, she's quite the showoff."

"She?" Mikah and I say together. I smile.

"Uh huh. Look." She points to the apex of the baby's thighs. There is nothing there to look at, just some more semi-transparent lines.

"There's nothing there," I say.

"Exactly," Dr. Alston says, pride in her voice. "You have a baby girl."

I smile and tears roll down my cheeks.

"A girl," I hear Mikah say through the device over my shoulder. His voice is soft, quiet, reverent.

I look over toward him and I see him staring at something. I'm assuming it's the monitor. Though he's not actually crying, I can tell by the look on his face that he is in awe.

I turn back to Dr. A., and she is back to pushing buttons. Sometimes the image freezes momentarily as she pushes a button.

I'm about to ask what she's doing when she says, "I'm assuming you'd like some more pictures."

"Yes, please."

After a few more clicks she pulls the wand away.

I turn back toward Mikah. He's wiping his eyes, not like he's wiping away tears, but rather like he's rubbing at them. I notice now that he looks very tired.

"How are you doing, Mikah?" I ask.

His hands come away and his head pops up a bit. "Thank you for letting me join you both for the ultrasound."

"Anytime," Dr. A. says. "I'll give you two a minute, and then I'll be back in." She walks around the bed, pulls the device out of its cradle and hands it to me.

I sit up and take hold of it.

As soon as the door clicks closed behind Dr. Alston, Mikah asks, "You okay?"

I nod. "It's just all so overwhelming sometimes. I wish you were here right now," I say. There is definite sadness in my voice, but also excitement. "How are you doing?"

"I'm fine. Was just up late last night dealing with some stuff." He smiles. I can tell that he's not wanting to go into details, which is okay with me. He quickly changes the subject. "A girl, huh?"

I smile. "I guess so." I can't stop the smile from spreading wider. "I was hoping, but you know..." I trail off. I had been hoping for a girl, but I didn't want to be let down.

"So you're happy?"

I cock my head at him, puzzled by his question. "Yes, though regardless, boy or girl, I'd be happy, so long as it were healthy."

He smiles. "Good. If I'd known that you wanted to know, I would have given you the envelope."

"No, it's okay. I'd forgotten about it until she brought it up again. Besides, she seems more sure now than she was when she gave us the envelope."

"True. What else has she said?"

"Not much. We talked about my aversion to red meat." He laughs at that. "She said it was normal for me to not like everything I may have liked before. She also asked about my vitamins and if I was taking them, and that was about as far as we got when you called."

"Okay, no more red meat. Got it." He laughs, teasing. "Can I call you tonight?"

My heart pounds. "When are you coming home?" I pause momentarily at what I've just said about home.

Mikah, on the other hand, doesn't quite catch it. "Tomorrow, in the morning. Early. I think. It's been pretty chaotic around here."

"I can tell, you look exhausted."

He snorts. "Yeah, I didn't sleep very well last night."

My brows knit together. "Why not?"

"We can talk about it later. I'm going to let you get back to your appointment. I'll call you when I'm done here, okay?"

"Okay. Thanks for joining us."

"No, thank you for letting me be a part of this."

I smile a little wider. "By the way, what is this thing that I'm talking to you on?" I ask.

"It's called an iPad. It's like your iPod, only bigger and a bit more sophisticated. Do you like it?"

"It's pretty cool, though all I've done is talk to you. Not sure what else it can do."

"I'll show you when I get home. Actually, I'll ask Celeste to show you the FaceTime app on your iPod. We can video chat tonight, if you'd like."

My heart patters a bit at the thought of seeing him again when we talk tonight, and I smile wide.

"Good. Alright, I wish you luck with the rest of your appointment, and I will talk to you soon."

"Okay, bye."

"Bye," he says.

The iPad beeps twice and he's gone.

Within a matter of seconds Dr. A. is back in the room.

"Thank you. For letting him call and join us." I say to her.

"You're welcome," she says and smiles.

I hand her back the iPad and she sets it down behind her. "Shall we finish this up?"

I nod and lie back down.

TWENTY-ONE

After about ten minutes, she's done doing whatever she needed to do down there. It didn't hurt exactly, but it was very uncomfortable.

"Everything looks fine. You're closer to eighteen weeks along and everything looks great."

I sit up. "Can I ask you something?" I say and blush.

She shakes a little in silent laughter, and an all-knowing smile spreads across her lips. "Of course."

"I'm wondering..." I can't seem to find the words I want to say.

"You're wondering about sex?"

Oh, God, is it really that obvious? The idea has crossed my mind once or twice over the last couple of weeks. I nod slowly, certain I've turned cherry red at this point.

"Don't be embarrassed, Vivienne. It's a perfectly natural question to ask, and every expectant mother asks the same question. The answer is yes, you can have sex."

I let out the breath I've been holding. "Can I ask you something else?"

"Anything, Vivienne."

"I'm not sure I want to know the answer to this, but I have to know..."

"The answer is no. When you came in the last time, I was deeply concerned about it too, so I checked almost immediately. There were no signs of trauma to indicate that."

I feel a tear streak down my face. I'd wanted to ask before I left the hospital two weeks ago, but it wasn't something I felt comfortable enough to ask. I'd healed so fast that I wasn't sure I would have noticed if Riley had succeeded in...

I can't even think the words.

"Thank you," I say quietly.

"Have you talked to anyone yet?"

I shake my head.

"It would probably be a good idea if you-"

"No, I don't want to talk to someone. I don't remember much about what happened to me, and I don't want to relive the memories that I do have over and over again while someone analyzes me. My past is my past. I can't change that fact. And I truly seem to be better about my reactions to certain things." I take a deep breath. "Andrew, the man outside, for example, doesn't scare me. Neither do Red or Connor, for that matter.

"Mikah is cautious, sometimes too cautious, but he'd figured out a lot of my triggers before. I've talked to him about it. Even a little bit about my past with Riley." I cringe internally at the name. "What happened with my mother is old history."

She is watching me carefully. "You're a strong woman, Vivienne. Don't ever let anyone tell you differently. I admire your courage and even your determination. But know that we can't always solve things on our own."

"I know, and Mikah has offered the same thing. I really just think that I've managed to process this all on my own, in my own way. Something I've always done."

She nods. "Okay then. I will leave it be, but know that I'm only a phone call away. If you need me for anything, all you have to do is call."

I smile and nod. "Thank you."

"You're welcome. How's your shoulder? And your wrist?"

I smile again at the change of subject. She knows when to stop, and I really like that about her.

"They're great. I don't have any problems moving my arm, and my wrist has been fine since I left here."

"Good. I will allow you to stop wearing the brace." Considering that I haven't been wearing it, until this morning, I try not to smile as she continues. "If you can, I'd recommend some light exercise, like walking. Or even yoga could be good for you. I will also allow you to return to work. However, I don't want you doing anything that requires you to be on your feet for long periods of time. So no waitressing."

Jeez, I hadn't even thought about the diner. Partly due to Mikah's vehement refusal to let me go back to work there.

"Talk to Mikah," Dr. Alston says. "He might have something for you, if you feel it's important to work. I would like to see you back here in a month. We will start regular monthly visits from here until closer to your due date."

"Speaking of due dates?"

She reaches into a drawer behind her. "Forty weeks is total time of pregnancy, give or take a week or two." I watch as she twists and turns the cardboard wheel in her hand. "April thirteenth."

I smile. "April thirteenth," I repeat. "I like it. But please tell me that's not a Friday?"

She laughs. "Superstitious?"

"Not really. But you know, it doesn't hurt to be cautious."

She laughs again and pulls out a calendar. "No, it's a Saturday."

"Good," I say and laugh.

TWENTY-TWO

When I emerge from the exam room, clothed and ready to go, Dr. Alston says, "All set?"

"Yeah."

She hands me a bag with a couple of things in it. "I've included another copy of the book I gave you, since you don't have the original one, and a few additional things about diet and such. To help with the lack of red meat." She winks at me.

I look in the bag. It's the book about how the body changes with pregnancy, the one left behind at my old apartment. "Oh that reminds me," I say. "I noticed this morning that, um, my breasts are swelling. A lot. To the point of painful."

"How painful?"

"Achy, really."

"That's pretty normal. A little early, but normal. Your breasts are beginning to produce colostrum. It's a form of breast milk. It's a thicker, creamier substance that is generally higher in fat and very good for the baby when she's born. Sometimes you can begin to leak early, which is okay. A good, supportive bra or sports bra can help alleviate some of the tenderness. Even wearing one at night can help. There are some tips in that book that might help. Plus..." she says as she turns back to her desk. She grabs a couple of pamphlets and brings them over to me. "Here are a couple of good information sources on some things you can do to be more comfortable. They will better explain that part of pregnancy."

I take them and slip them into the bag. "Thank you. For everything."

"Anytime, Vivienne. Anything. I'll see you in a month."

"See you then." I reach for and turn the knob on the door.

Andrew is standing in front of the door, but he moves away quickly as I step through.

"Thanks again, Dr. Alston," I say over my shoulder.

She waves and Andrew whisks me down the hall. He reaches for his phone. "On our way," he says as we round the corner back toward the parking garage.

TWENTY-THREE

I hop into the shower shortly after arriving home from my appointment. When I come out, Celeste is in the kitchen. She is standing over the sink, washing dishes. The first couple of times she was here cleaning and doing dishes and such, I offered to help, but she would hear none of that.

Celeste is awesome to be around. She's very funny and down to earth, and I'm comfortable with having her here. She talks about her boyfriend all the time, and I get the distinct impression that they are head-over-heels in love with each other.

"Hi, Celeste," I say as I take a seat at the breakfast bar.

"Hi, Vivienne. How was your appointment?"

I smile because she remembered. She really misses nothing about what's going on around her.

"It was good. Mikah called in and we used...an iPad?" I say, puzzled. "He was able to watch the whole thing."

"That's awesome. Those iPads are amazing."

"I'd never seen one before. But it was nice to have him there without him being there. He said he was going to get in touch with you, ask you to show me how to use FaceTime?" I think that's what he called it.

"That was nice of him. I haven't heard from him yet, but I can certainly show you on your iPod," she says sweetly. "So did you find anything out?"

"Like?" I say, confused.

"Did you find out what you're having?"

"Oh, yes." I smile. She looks at me expectantly and I laugh. "It's a girl."

She bounces up and down, clapping, excitement radiating off of her. I can't help but laugh at her girlish behavior.

"You're having a girl. Oh, Viv, I'm so excited for you."

I smile. "Me, too." And for the first time, I really do feel deep-down excitement about being pregnant and the fact that it's going to be a girl.

She settles down some, but I can tell that she's still really excited. "What would you like to eat?" she asks.

I roll my eyes, but my stomach growls. "Peanut butter and jelly?" I say.

She smiles. "Alright, coming right up."

"I can make it," I say, knowing full well that she will shoot me down.

"Oh, no. That's my job."

I shake my head as she gets busy. I climb off of the chair and head toward the living room.

One of the things that I hate about not working is the fact that I just sit around doing nothing. Celeste handles all the cleaning in my apartment, all the laundry, and even the majority of the cooking. What she doesn't cook, Mikah does. Well, he heats up things that she's made, but his easy manner in the kitchen tells me that he is more than capable of cooking a meal on his own.

I wonder idly about the diner. About Laura especially, and how she's doing. I haven't thought about any of that since the attack because, well...the dream I had right before leaving the hospital. I don't know if that's now or in the future, and it scares me. I haven't called the diner because if Nyssa really is in cahoots with Riley, the less they know, the better. I make a mental note to ask Mikah if he ever told them about what happened to me.

I grab my journal off of the coffee table and take a seat on the couch. I'd been avoiding this since Red brought it back to me from my apartment. It's just another reminder of my old apartment and what happened. I guess it was my way of dealing with the whole mess.

At the push of a button on the remote, my iPod flickers to life in its cradle. A beautiful instrumental piece starts to play as I open up my journal. The money I stored in it falls out. I'd forgotten all about this being in here. Plus there are the food stamp vouchers. Jeez, and W.I.C., too. Dang it, what am I going to do with all this stuff? I could give it to Celeste to use when she goes shopping, but I hardly see that as necessary.

I tuck the vouchers into the back of the journal and decide to put the money in my purse.

Where is my purse? Wow, I really hadn't thought about a lot of this stuff.

"Celeste?"

"Yes, Vivienne?" she calls back from the kitchen.

"Do you know where...or, if Red managed to recover my purse from my apartment?"

She stops what she's doing, almost as if she's recalled something she hadn't intended to remember. "Um, Red found it, but..." She pauses, looking at me, concern etched in her features. "I threw it out because it, um..."

Well, shit. "It's alright. What about my wallet and the stuff inside?"

She lightens up a little at my response. "That I do have. I'll run up to Mikah's and get it for you." She hurries to finish making my lunch.

I loved that bag and I'm sad to see it go, but I'm happier that I've been sheltered from seeing it covered in blood.

I shudder.

"Here you go." Celeste is standing behind the couch with my sandwich on a plate.

"Thank you," I say as I reach up and take it from her.

"You're welcome. I'll be back down in a bit."

"My wallet is no rush," I say, assuming that's why she's rushing upstairs.

"Okay, but I need to go take care of a few things upstairs, anyway. I'll let you eat in peace, and I'll be back down in a bit. Would you like to go shopping for a new purse this afternoon?"

Normally I would reject the idea, but I have the money from my journal. "I'd love to," I say with enthusiasm, and her face lights up.

"Perfect. I'll let the guys know, and when you're done eating, come on upstairs, if you'd like, or I'll be back in about an hour."

"Okay." I nod.

She turns to leave and is about a third of the way to the door when I stop her. "Celeste?"

"Yes?" She stops and turns toward me.

"Can you help me find something for Mikah while we're out?" I ask shyly. I'd like to give him something to thank him for all he's done for me, though I have no clue what.

She smiles. "Of course."

I smile back and she heads for the door. As she opens it, I can see Andrew and Connor in the hallway, talking. They turn to Celeste as she shuts the door.

TWENTY-FOUR

About halfway through the second half of my sandwich, the phone rings. I expect it to be Celeste from upstairs, but when I look at the handset I see Mikah's name and my heart flutters.

I swallow the bite that's in my mouth and click the green button. "Hello."

"Hey, beautiful," he says with enthusiasm.

I smile at his endearment. "Hi, Mikah. How are you?"

He laughs a little bit. "I'm good, how are you doing?"

"I'm great. Just finished eating a sandwich."

"Peanut butter and jelly?"

I laugh. "How'd you know?"

"Because it's what you always eat." He has a point there. "Listen, Celeste sent me a text. You want to go shopping?"

Uh, crap. "Yes, I just found out that she threw out my purse because it, um, was in my apartment." I don't need to say any more. "Though the shopping was her idea."

He chuckles. "I know it was. At my urging, though she didn't expect you to be enthusiastic about it."

"I'm not sure that I'm excited about it. I'm not much of a shopper. But I..." I debate with myself about whether to tell him about my own money. In the end I decide to be

106

honest with him. "I finally opened my journal, and I had money stashed in there. So I'd like to get a new purse." I brace myself.

"I think you getting a new purse is a great idea. But-" Yup, here it comes. "-I've already arranged for a shopping budget for you-"

"Mikah, that's not necessary. I have some money-"

"Please, Vivienne, can I explain?"

I sigh. "Yes."

"I arranged the budget about a week ago. I wanted you to be able to..." He pauses. I hear him take a deep breath. "I wanted you to be able to buy things for yourself. And for the baby. I knew that your not working would mean you couldn't buy the things you need or want without my or Celeste's intervention."

I think I'm maybe starting to understand. He continues, "There are certain things that I know you're going to need or want that wouldn't have been the easiest things to ask for, so I thought if I arranged a way for you to get them on your own, you wouldn't have to ask."

I immediately think about the conversation that Dr. A. and I had this morning about sports bras and such. Surely a budget from Mikah isn't necessary, though. A sports bra and a purse can't really be that expensive, right?

"Vivienne?" he says quietly, bracing for my reaction.

"I...I'm just processing this. Give me a moment. I'm really trying to not be angry at you."

"My cute little tiger," he says coyly.

I smile at his tone. "What's that mean?"

"You're like a tiger trapped in a cat's body, just waiting for the moment to strike."

There is a undertone of adoration in his voice that surprises me. I actually laugh. "Well, Mikah, I've learned to expect the unexpected with you. No, I'm not happy about it. No, I don't really plan to use your money. But sometimes I feel that the argument is old because you know how I feel about it." I sigh. "You've given me so much already - a place to live, food, clothes - and it is very hard for me to accept those things from you when I have nothing to give you in return."

"That's not true. You give me everything, Vivienne."

"What's that supposed to mean?" I ask, surprised.

"I- Look, I really don't want to have this conversation on the phone. I would much rather do it in person. Can we discuss this when I get home tomorrow?" His voice is shaky, betraying nervousness.

"Yeah, we can talk about it tomorrow," I say, but the reluctance I feel is obvious in my voice.

"How did the rest of your appointment with Dr. Alston go?"

I roll my eyes at the sudden change in subject, but I also smile. "She's giving me clearance to go back to work, and I no longer have to wear the wrist brace."

"That's good." He pauses, from the past encounters we've had, when he's wanted something, this happens. I play with the hem of my shirt, waiting patiently for him to decide what he wants to ask me. "What if...what if I asked you not to go back to work?"

I try very hard not to roll my eyes. This isn't the first time we've had discussions about working, though he's never been so blunt about it. "Mikah, that's kind of important to my own sanity and survival. What am I going to do around here all day long? Celeste cleans and cooks everything, and I get bored easily. The only reason I've managed to stay sane so far is because you've been here. With you gone, I'm going stir crazy."

He sighs. "I know. But what if I could give you something to do all day, or at least part of the day?"

"What are you getting at, Mikah?"

"What if you could go back to school?"

"What?" I say, shocked. Going to college has always been something I've strongly desired - doing something with my brain - but it's always been out of reach. "What makes you think that's something I want to do? And even if I did want to, I can't afford it." I immediately regret that last part. I know dang well that he intends to pay for it.

"I'd take care of that, and I'm pretty sure that you'd be very good at school."

"What makes you think that?"

He takes a deep breath. "You're brilliant and..." He pauses. "I know what you scored on your SATs."

I roll my eyes again. "What *don't* you know about me, Mikah?" I knew from the first time he took me to the hospital that he'd pried into my past so I'm not entirely surprised that he knows my SAT scores, but it still bugs me that he's done this kind of research on me.

Then again, I researched him. Just not in as much detail.

"I don't know you," he says, "though I'm learning more and more each day."

"Can I think about it?" I reply.

"Of course. But if you don't want to go to school and you insist on going to work, would you allow me to offer you a job at my firm?"

"Doing what, Mikah? I have no skills or experience working in an office." Honestly, what could I do at his office that I would have even clue one about doing?

"Well, I have a couple of intern and entry-level positions open that I could offer you. You could learn. I have no doubt that whatever you put your mind to you will be brilliant at." I can hear the excitement in his voice.

"Listen, we can talk about this some more this weekend. I don't expect you to decide right now. Okay?"

"Alright." I sigh. "When are you coming home?"

"Do you miss me?"

"Yes."

I hear his sharp intake of breath at my words.

"Why does that surprise you?" I ask.

"Because. I miss you, too."

I smile.

"I will be home tomorrow, hopefully in the morning. Viv, I wanted to ask you something else."

"What's that?"

"Tomorrow night there is a charity gala that I'm supposed to attend. I'd like it if you would be my date."

"Uh..." I'm taken aback by his question, surprised that he would want to take me to something like that. "Mikah, I've never been to anything like that before." I pull my feet up, cross my legs and lean back into the couch. I place my hand on my belly and begin rubbing it.

"I know, but it's really no big thing. We go, have dinner, there is an auction, and dinner is followed by a dance. It's a stuffed shirt, black tie kind of thing. I am not a fan of going to them, but this one is for an important charity that I've been a part of since its inception, so it is really important that I be there. I just don't want to go without you."

I'm pondering his words as I continue to stroke my belly. "I have nothing to wear," I say, and he chuckles.

"Does that mean you'll go?"

I roll my eyes at his enthusiasm. "Yes, Mikah, I'll go."

"Yes! Okay, I will have Celeste make some arrangements for you to have a nice, relaxing day tomorrow, get your hair done, be pampered a little. And when you guys go out today, you can find yourself a dress." The excitement in his voice is infectious, and I can't help but smile.

I splay my hand across my belly, and as I do, I feel something, almost like bubbles under my hand. "Holy crap."

"I'm sure you'll-"

"No, not that." I cut him off. I rub at my belly again, placing a little more pressure on it, and it happens again. "Whoa."

"Vivienne, what's the matter?"

I feel tears on my cheeks. "I-" It hits again. "I think she's moving. It feels like little bubbles."

"Vivienne, are you serious?" he says with major excitement in his voice.

I laugh a choked laugh. "Yes, I'm serious. It feels so..." I can't think of the words.

"Viv, that's so...wow."

My thoughts exactly.

TWENTY-FIVE

Not long after I get off the phone with Mikah, Andrew comes into the apartment, hands me an envelope and tells me that Celeste will be down shortly. The envelope has some papers and something flat and hard inside. I open it up.

Inside is a letter and a black and silver credit card that says *American Express Elite* and has my name on it. Holy shit, his damn shopping budget involves a credit card.

I open up the letter. At first I think it's handwritten, but when I run my fingers over it I realize it's been printed in a font that looks just like his handwriting.

Dearest Vivienne,

In this envelope you will find your very own credit card. Please do not be mad at me, but after our conversation today, I wanted you to be able to go out and go shopping with Celeste with your own credit card.

Andrew and Connor will accompany both of you, and I've reserved some private shopping time at Neiman Marcus to cut back on security concerns. Please make sure that you also pick up a coat or two, one for tomorrow night and one for everyday use. While I love seeing you in my Boston College sweatshirt, it is hardly warm enough for the weather.

I hope you enjoy your shopping. Once again I'm awed by the fact that I've been able to be a part of yet another milestone in your pregnancy.

I cannot wait to see you tomorrow.

Be Safe,
M

By the time I'm done reading the note, I'm over the fact that he insists on paying for my shopping. He's actually given me a list of the things he would like me to buy, which makes it a little easier to take the credit card, though I'm not sure I'll feel right using it for anything other than what he's outlined.

Neiman Marcus turns out to be a beast of a store – huge and full of everything and rather overwhelming. However, I do manage to find a dress for tomorrow night. I'm shocked beyond measure when I see it. It's too perfect and I'm able to wear it, pregnant belly and all, without purchasing a maternity dress. Celeste comments at one point that, despite my belly, my small frame will allow me to wear regular style clothing for some time before I really have to get into the maternity styles. I'm relieved to hear it because I'm not all that impressed with the maternity section in the store.

I also manage to find shoes and a coat for tomorrow night that actually match the dress, as well as a coat for everyday use. I also pick up two bras from the maternity section; when I try them on, the soft, supportive fabric brings nearly instant relief.

Purses are a whole other issue. Neiman Marcus doesn't have a single purse that I like within my price range, but when I ask Celeste if we can just go to Target or Wal-Mart, she looks at me like I've lost my mind. Eventually I find one that I really like for day-to-day use. Then I find a second one that's white and matches my dress for tomorrow night. It's smaller and fancier, definitely not for everyday use. I refuse to look at the price tags on them as we head toward the register.

Celeste does her best to encourage me to buy more things, but I'm determined to use Mikah's credit card only for the things that he's pointed out.

When we're done, we head home. I'm exhausted from all of the day's events and very thankful that Celeste is making me dinner because I don't have the energy.

Just as I sit down to eat, Mikah calls my iPod using FaceTime, and Celeste shows me how to use it. Mikah's exhausted, too. We cut the conversation short because his flight out of Phoenix is leaving early in the morning.

After dinner, I curl up on the couch to watch a movie, but before I know it, my eyelids become heavy. I manage to turn off the TV and stumble into the bedroom before falling into a deep sleep.

TWENTY-SIX

The next morning I wake up early, around seven, rub the sleep from my eyes, and shuffle into the bathroom to take a shower. As I shed my clothing I notice something strange about the way I'm moving, but I can't quite place it.

That's when I catch a glimpse of myself in the mirror and start to scream. I quickly clasp my hand over my mouth, remembering that one of the men is standing outside the door to the apartment.

"Calm down, angel."

"How in the hell am I supposed to calm down? Look at me!"

"I know. Breathe. We will handle this together," the female voice says calmly.

I don't even bother to look around; I know she's not in the room to be seen. No, she's in my head.

What the hell was I dreaming about?

"Elysium, and, erm..."

Well, crap, so dreaming about Elysium is now causing my wings to sprout? I thought I only had wings while I was in Elysium, not...

I trail off. It's obvious right now that my assumption was incorrect, as I'm staring at wings - smaller than those in Elysium, but still wings - sprouting from my back. They are about a quarter of the size of those in my dreams.

I'd already managed to shed my tank top before I'd realized that these beautiful white wings with silvery trim were pushing their way out, and my naked torso, framed by my flaming red, curly hair and white wings is, well, breathtakingly beautiful. The image is actually quite-

"Angels do not think such things."

I blush at her catching the direction of my thoughts, but I say, "Can you blame me?"

She laughs, the sound like a chorus of angels singing and bells ringing. "No, my child, I do not and cannot blame you for such thoughts."

I suddenly have a mental image of her fanning herself, and I shake my head.

Looking back into the mirror, I almost don't want the wings to go away. But I'm not sure how on earth I will explain this to Celeste, let alone the men and Mikah.

"Mikah knows."

"Wait, what? How?" I've suspected that we share the dreams together, but not that he actually knows.

"Well, he has an idea. He is the one that noticed your back first. In the hospital."

"Why hasn't he said anything?"

I feel her shrug. "More than likely, he is trying not to scare you. And he isn't the only one aware of what you are."

"Wait a minute. Who else knows?"

"Your guardians know." She's playing coy and it's starting to piss me off.

"Spill it, Zirah. Who the hell else knows about this?" As I say this, I watch my wings flare, almost like they're taking a big breath.

"Celeste."

My eyes bulge and my mouth drops open.

"Andrew, Connor, and..." She stops.

"Red?" I whisper the last name.

"Yes," she says.

"Does Mikah know this?"

"No. He suspects, but he doesn't know for certain that he is not the only one protecting you. The others are something different. They are not angels, but guardians of Elysium. They have abilities of protection that you and Mikah do not. They act as shields, especially for you. They are more like assistants to Mikah. They are able to regenerate and to morph into anything that you may need for protection, though they also have their limitations."

I take a deep breath, trying to take all of this in. Since stepping out of those hospital doors two weeks ago, I've been more protected than I ever could've thought possible. Having guards outside the door was one thing, but knowing that those guards are really doing more than I can imagine is...

"They've been able to hide you from detection. While the ones who wish to harm you cannot detect you, your being alive has prevented the *foinse olc* – or source of evil, the devil - from returning to his full strength. This is the reason that Riley tried to kill you. Though he has his own personal reasons for wanting you dead, he is operating on the command of the devil. He has failed, and is failing, and it is only a matter of time before *he* has his way with him."

"How so?" I breathe.

"He will take Riley into the inner circles of Hades."

I'm reminded of our earlier conversation about Dante's *Inferno*. There are levels of hell in that book.

"You're not far off. That story is surprisingly accurate. Killing you was to be Riley's rite of passage. He was to be one of the devil's minions, part of his demon circle. Riley's failure is your gain, and he will soon be doomed to relive torture day in and day out."

I shiver and watch as my wings shimmer in the light of the bathroom.

"Okay. Can you make these things go away?" I manage to mumble.

"Yes, my angel, but I would like to teach you how to bring them in. It's actually rather simple. All you need to do is visualize them coming back in, and they will retract of their own accord."

I close my eyes to avoid being distracted by the sight of them in the mirror. I flex my shoulders and can feel them move from deep inside. I focus on that feeling and imagine pulling them in. The process is slow, but little by little I feel them settling in on my back.

Once I feel that they are back in place, I slowly open my eyes. They're gone. All that is left in the mirror is me. I sigh. I rather enjoyed seeing my wings in person for the first time, but I'm glad to have them tucked away.

TWENTY-SEVEN

After my shower, I put on one of my new bras and am excited by the fact that my breasts are not as sore. I still feel the tight heaviness and it's mildly uncomfortable, but it's manageable.

Once I'm dressed, I head out into the living room. Surprisingly, Celeste is nowhere to be found, but on the breakfast bar is a bagel, spread thickly with strawberry cream cheese, and a card.

I shuffle toward it and take a seat. Picking up the card, I read:

Good morning, Vivienne. I've left this bagel for you. I will be back around 9:15 to collect you. Mikah has arranged a day at the spa just for you.
Enjoy! Celeste.

The spa? What the hell is that? I shrug and pick up my bagel, taking a huge bite.

When I'm done eating, I still have about twenty minutes before she will be back. I take to transferring the minimal contents of my old wallet to the new one, which matches my new black purse. It is round on the bottom and flat at the top. Celeste called it "bucket style." She was careful to remove the tag so I wouldn't see the price, but it is covered in silhouettes of the letter *C*. The wallet is the same material and color. She tried to convince me to get another color, but I preferred the black one.

I also put my journal in my new bag, along with a few of the other things, chapstick, a tattered picture of my mother and a gentleman, whom my mother said is my father and a small package of Kleenex, that Celeste saved from my old one. I pause a moment to look at the picture again. There is something strangely familiar about the man next to my mother, but I can't place him. I take one last look at my old wallet, I toss it into the garbage under the coffee table. I won't need it anymore.

I grab my new bag and set it up on the breakfast bar, waiting for Celeste to show up.

The phone rings. My heart pounds as it occurs to me it might be Mikah. Then I scowl, remembering he was leaving early this morning and should be on a plane. But when I pick it up off of its cradle and look at it, I see that it is Mikah.

"Good morning," I say enthusiastically into the phone.

There's no answer on the other end of the line.

"Hello?" I say again. Nothing. For reasons unknown the wings on my back buzz. "Mikah, are you there?"

Still no answer.

I turn toward the door to the apartment and jump, dropping the phone. Standing in the doorway is Mikah with his phone to his ear.

"Gah! Don't do that to me," I say, but he's just standing there.

My back is ablaze. Fear strikes through me, and I suddenly understand that this is not Mikah. My wings begin to push out from my back and into my top,

120

straining against the material. I hear the seams starting to rip, and the next thing I know, the shirt is no longer tight but shredded and falling away from my body.

Whatever is standing in the doorway is staring hard at me, its gaze intense.

Inside my head I start yelling for help, but what I'm screaming isn't English.

Suddenly, out of nowhere, Andrew is standing between me and the figure in the door. He is poised and ready to take on whatever it is, but he's puzzled by what he's seeing.

"Blake," Andrew says.

The man's eyes do not waver from me.

My wings flap hard, once, twice, harder and faster each time, sending waves of air past and around me. I feel lighter on my feet, but before I can actually take off, Red appears in front of me.

"Do not take off. You are safe, no harm will come to you."

He turns around, and suddenly all the air my wings have produced is pushing back at me, almost like I'm in front of a wall, and Red has disappeared. The scene in front of me shimmers and ripples as if I'm looking through a fishbowl. I can still see the room, though, and I watch the eyes of the man at the door as they shift, searching.

Connor appears behind him. So quickly that I can't follow it, Connor has his arms around the man's neck and Andrew attacks from the front.

Andrew strikes, throwing a punch at the man's gut, not once but three or four times. Then he spins him out of Connor's grasp and into his own.

"Who are you?" I hear Andrew growl. His voice is deep, scary and demonic. The muscles in his back shift as he strains harder against the man in his arms.

Connor is on him fast with a blade at least six inches long pointed at his chest. "I will run you through. Who are you? What are you doing here?"

The figure in Andrew's arms shifts and morphs. His skin takes on a darker tone, almost black, mixed with green. His hair disappears and...horns?

"Jesus, a shifter." Connor spats. "Who sent you?"

"Who do you think? I've come for her. I've come to take her to Him," the demon snarls the last word.

"I don't think so," Andrew says, and in one fast move he's turned the shifter around and pushed him to the floor. Andrew's legs are entangled with the intruder's and his hands are pressing hard into his shoulders.

Before I can even worry about the fact that the demon's hands are free, Connor is on them, holding them down as Andrew reaches inside his boot and withdraws another six-inch knife. This one looks like it's made out of gold.

"Take her, now!" Andrew shouts at Red.

In an instant I'm engulfed in a bubble-like shell, and then I'm standing in a solid white room, much like the room from my dreams. Elysium.

TWENTY-EIGHT

My heart races and blood pulses behind my ears. I can't even begin to imagine how I've managed to get here, let alone so quickly.

I pinch my arm. "Ouch!" Nope, I'm not dreaming.

"What the hell just happened?" I nearly scream.

"Calm down, Vivienne, no need to get worked up. That was a shifter."

"How did he get past Andrew and Connor?" Come to think of it: "And how did you get here? You're supposed to be with Mikah."

Red takes a seat on the white couch. His face wears a soft expression that I find comforting. "I'll explain it all," he says. "Have a seat, take a breath. You're alright, and we'll discuss it."

I start to pace.

"Vivienne, please, sit. Everyone is fine. No one is harmed." I try to sit, but I can't, at least not in a chair. My wings are still in full extension. I take a seat on the bench opposite the couch.

"Shifters are something of an in-between. They are not exactly human, but they are not demonic, either." I never noticed Red's accent before, but the more he talks, the more I hear it. "They have the ability to travel between

123

realms, but the catch is that they can only project themselves. They are not actually present until they complete their transition. They project to an area where they want to be, which in this case was the end of the ringing line. Where you were. When you answered the phone he honed in on your position and projected to it."

"But he looked like Mikah," I say, completely breathless.

"He took the shape of something you wouldn't run from." He twirls his wedding band around his finger. "He needed you to keep the connection open long enough for him to fully teleport into the room. That's when Andrew and Connor intercepted. There's an alarm system in the house to warn us of intruders, but it doesn't always detect shifters when in their projected form. He pauses to take a deep breath. "When he tried to complete his teleport, it set off all the alarms and connected to my phone. When it went off, I came as fast as I could. I shielded you so that the shifter couldn't see you when he teleported into the house. He'd be confused, allowing us to take him down as we did."

I look up at him, confused. Then Zirah's words from earlier come back. "Shields?" I whisper.

"Yes, darlin'. All of us - Andrew, Connor and myself - have the ability to create a camouflage of sorts that will turn anything behind it invisible."

I put my head in my hands. "This is all...it's too much."

"Breathe. You're safe, and your location is still undetected."

My head snaps up. "You're joking, right? He was in the apartment."

"No, his image was. All this one saw was the inside of an apartment, but the location of that apartment is covered up by the securities we have in place. Think of him as a hologram."

"A what?"

"It's like a three-dimensional picture. You can see it, but if you touch it there is nothing there. Shifters are different from holograms in the sense that they shift into the dimension they're after, and though they are not solid, certain supreme beings have the ability to touch - or make physical contact with - and control them. Myself, Andrew and Connor are three of those people.

"The location is safe because your shifter was unable to move, unable to fully shift into the apartment because of the protection we have in place."

"So now I have to worry about holograms showing up in the apartment."

"No," says a voice behind me. I turn to the sound and it is Andrew.

"Gah! Jesus, stop that, would you?"

"Sorry." He looks from me to Red. "We're in the clear." He looks cautiously at me then back to Red. "It's been taken care of."

I need no more explanation from him; I know what he is saying without him actually saying it.

"We've added additional protection to the building, especially the apartments."

"Aaron?" Red says.

"Aye, he's taking care of it."

"Wait a minute, who's Aaron?" I interrupt them.

Andrew kneels down next to me. "Are you okay?"

"Who's Aaron?" I repeat.

The way he shakes his head gives me the distinct impression that Mikah has done a thorough briefing with him about my stubbornness.

"Aaron is another one of us, but he has the ability to provide an additional protection, the ability to stop shifters from coming into an area that's protected by him. He's placing protection on the building, as well as on you. No matter where you go, you'll be safe."

I feel a knot of stress form in my back and my wings respond by quivering.

"Can you pull them back in?" Red asks.

I look at him and my wings twitch. "I think so. Though I've only done it once."

Red cannot hide the shock on his face. Obviously that was not something he was expecting to hear.

"I sort of woke up with them this morning. That's how I found out about what you guys are. Which is why I'm not so much shocked by what you've done, but rather by that thing finding me in the first place."

Andrew chimes in. "I'm not convinced he knows what he found for certain. Red was quick with the shield, and we've taken care of him so he cannot return and report."

"I just need to know that I'm safe and that this won't happen to me again."

"No, ma'am," Andrew says.

I scowl at him but I don't want to fight right now about him calling me Vivienne, so instead I focus on reining in my wings. I lower my head to my hands, placing the heels of my palms against my eyes and closing them tight, and I concentrate on my wings.

TWENTY-NINE

After I manage to pull myself back together, Andrew leads me to a door opposite where we were sitting and I magically walk back into the apartment. It looks exactly as it did when I answered the phone.

I need a serious amount of something to process all of this. It's just too much.

Connor and Celeste are in the apartment when Andrew and I walk in. Red doesn't follow us.

"Where's Red?" I ask.

"He went back to Mikah. They're on their way home," Connor says.

I nod. "Now what?" I say.

Celeste steps forward. "Now you have a spa appointment."

"You're kidding, right?" I retort.

"Nope. Come on, grab your stuff," she says.

"Please tell me you're joking. After that?" I say back.

Connor speaks up. "Mikah does not know about this, about you, or about us. Proceeding with the day as planned is the best way to keep it that way."

"Why is hiding who and what you are from Mikah so important?" I ask.

They all look at each other. Andrew is the one who answers. "Mikah can and will know about us, but him finding out about a shifter here will send him over the edge. We are just trying to take it slower on him." He pauses. "He is having a harder time adjusting to what he is than you are."

I look at all of them, puzzled. "I'm not sure I'm handling any of this, to be honest."

They all laugh, just a little.

"Yeah, you are," Celeste says. "You've yet to freak out."

I laugh. "I guess it is just a matter of accepting my fate. It is what it is, and until it affects me to the point of spending every day in Elysium or in fear of someone or something getting to me, I'm not sure there is much I can do about it." I also take into consideration that the one person I seem to want to spend all my time with is just like me. But I don't tell them that.

"That is a beautiful attitude. I wish we all had that kind of outlook when we found out." Celeste is still smiling as she says this. "That is how we know that you can handle this more than Mikah can. Eventually he will step into his own role. We just need to give him time."

I nod. "Okay, then. I guess we're going to a spa?"

THIRTY

A little over three hours later we arrive back at the underground garage of the condo. Andrew and Connor are both there to escort me into the elevator. However, neither one of them join me on my way up to my floor. When the doors open, Red is in the hallway.

"Good afternoon and welcome home, Ms. Vivienne."

"Thank you, Red. Is he home?"

"Yes, ma'am. He's inside waiting for you."

"Thank you."

I'm immediately surprised when I walk in: Lining the hallway are candles about every three feet. They've been placed so nicely that they almost look like they've been there forever.

I don't see Mikah anywhere, but I can hear the shower in the guest bathroom. He must be in there. I pause by the door, tempted to open it and let him know I'm here, but decide against it.

Instead I follow the path of candles to the breakfast bar. Sitting atop the bar is a vase containing two roses: a beautiful red rose in full bloom and a baby Fire and Ice rose. I smile. Next to the vase with the roses sits a package that looks similar to the one that contained the original Baby Callahan picture. A note on top says *Open Me* in Mikah's script.

I pick it up and rip open the paper to reveal a black box. I pull the top off, and looking back at me is a silver frame engraved with the words *It's a Girl* along the top and *Baby Callahan, taken November 9th, 2012* at the bottom. The frame is empty. I remember the ultrasound pictures Dr. Alston gave me yesterday and I know the perfect one.

I head over to the coffee table, bypassing the other candles. I'd like to put the picture in this frame before Mikah gets out of the bathroom so he can see it.

Grabbing the envelope off of the table, I flip to the one of her beautiful profile and lift the frame from the box. I'm surprised to find another frame underneath, this one an exact duplicate of the one he gave me before, picture and all. He's given me back my picture.

I slide the picture into the first frame and stand it up next to the vase, then pick up the other frame and set it up on the other side.

I'm about to throw the box away when I notice that it contains another, smaller box, a black velvet one. It's a jewelry box. Puzzled, I open the lid hesitantly and gasp.

Inside is a silver bracelet. It has a small heart locket near the clasp. Hooked onto the heart is a pair of miniature baby booties with pink gems on them. It's beautiful.

I slip the bracelet onto my wrist and I'm instantly in love with the way it looks and the way it feels. It is, of course, too much, but it is something that he's actually thought about, like the frames. And it symbolizes our baby girl.

Whoa, did I...? Yeah, I did. But I'm surprised to find that, rather than feeling really awkward, I take comfort in the idea of *our*.

I look at the bracelet as it sparkles in the shimmering light of the candles throughout the apartment.

After a few moments I pull the box off the counter, again intending to throw it away, and this time I spot a card taped to the counter underneath where the box sat.

Leave the box. There is something else waiting for you in the bedroom.

I notice now that the shower has stopped, and I get a tingling feeling that Mikah has been watching me from the bathroom. I smile but don't turn around as I head off toward my bedroom.

THIRTY-ONE

Stepping over the threshold into my bedroom, I notice that there are no candles in here but that the lights are on and dimmed. Lying on the bed are three boxes: one huge, one about the size of a shoe box, and one smaller still.

"Mikah, what have you done?"

The biggest one says *Open first* across the top. I smile and pull the paper-wrapped lid back to find pink tissue paper.

I slowly pull the paper back.

And gasp.

Any doubts that Mikah has been sharing my dreams with me are swept away. Inside the box is the very same dress that I've been wearing in our dream: the white tank top dress with silver accents beneath the chest and atop my baby bump. The straps are accented with the same design at the top. These accents hold the flowing gossamer train. The back is wide open, allowing room for my wings if they were out.

Peeling my eyes away from the first box, I sidestep to box number two.

Tears prick my eyes as I pull the lid off the box. Inside is a pair of white ballerina slippers that have long ribbons attached, no doubt to wrap around my calves. They're very pretty.

Finally, box number three.

These belonged to my mother.

I cover my mouth to hold in my gasp. Why would he give me something from his mother? Do I really mean that much to him? Then I remember our dream. Yes, I think I do.

I slowly open the last box and slide back the tissue paper. Sitting upon a shiny material are two bracelets. The bands that I'm wearing in the dream. In the center of the swirls are the white pearls. Also sitting among the material is what appears to be a headband of sorts, or a tiara.

My fingers gently glide along the smooth silver.

"You don't need to wear it all tonight."

I don't jump because I've had a feeling he was watching me. "I don't know what to say."

"Say you'll wear it."

I nod my head enthusiastically. "Of course I will."

I turn around to face him. He is standing there barefoot, in dress pants, no shirt, and his hair is still wet and dripping slightly.

The sight of him has me weak in the knees, but a huge weight dissolves almost the instant that I look into his bright, brilliant blue eyes.

"Hi, beautiful," he says and smiles that gorgeous smile he has that no doubt has the ability to bring any woman to her knees.

"Hi," I breathe.

He makes no move toward me, so I cross the room to him and throw my arms around his chest. I accidentally touch the wings on his back, and a tremor runs through his body.

He wraps his arms around me and kisses the top of my head.

"I missed you," I mumble into his chest.

"I can tell. I missed you, too."

He rubs along my back, and my body shakes in response. A desire to be closer to him grows hot within my body and it frightens me. I don't have a clue what this means. I've never felt anything like it before.

"You look beautiful," he says quietly.

"Thank you."

"You're welcome. Now, we need to leave in about twenty minutes. Will you be ready?"

I nod into his chest once again and he pulls back slightly.

"Good. Now we both need to get dressed," he says, kissing the top of my head again and pulling free of my arms.

I reluctantly let him go.

He turns toward the other bedroom and I see his beautiful wings shimmering across his back, vivid and alive.

THIRTY-TWO

I change quickly, starting with the shoes. I slide them onto my feet and crisscross the laces up each calf. Standing straight again, I replace the tan bra I'm wearing - which would've worked well for the dress I'd planned to wear - for a white, lacy one. I also pull on a pair of white lace boy shorts to match. I'm relieved to notice that although the back of the dress is open, it will still cover up my bra.

I slip easily into the dress and guide one bracelet over each of my wrists. I cannot bear to part with the locket he gave me earlier, so I decide to leave it on, too.

I cannot help but smile at the beautiful woman staring back at me in the full-length mirror. She is elegant, graceful, and classically beautiful. With her hair pulled back off of her face and cascading down her back, she looks like Cinderella, ready for the ball.

I'm overcome by the idea of what people will think, seeing me on Mikah's arm. I will become the center of attention; I can feel it already.

"Get a grip," I say quietly to myself. I've never cared what anyone has thought of me. Why start now?

I feel a tingle of excitement right as the knock comes. "Viv, it's almost time to go."

"I'll be right there," I say back loudly.

I reach for the little purse I bought yesterday to go with the dress I'd originally planned to wear. That dress is similar to this one, but it will sit unused in the closet. I wonder if Celeste can return it for me.

I sneak one final sideways glance at myself in the mirror. My bump is more pronounced from this angle, but for some strange reason, it's a very welcome sight.

When I step out from the bedroom, I see Mikah standing at the breakfast bar with his back to me. The candles are still lit, but the light over the bar is on. He's changed his pants. He's now wearing white pants.

I take a few steps in his direction and he turns toward me. As he turns I see that a thick silver stripe runs up the outside of his pants and that he is wearing a silver vest and tie under his white jacket.

I can't help the fascinated smile that spreads across my face at the fact that we match.

"Hello, beautiful," he says, and I blush. Not from his words but because I actually feel beautiful.

He walks toward me, his eyes raking me up and down, taking me in. The dress covers my feet completely. Only he and I will know that I wear only skimpy ballet slippers on my feet.

"You look gorgeous," he breathes.

The desire to kiss him is burning through my body, and I can't help but look up at him, hoping that maybe he'll finally kiss my lips.

But he goes for my forehead instead. Ever the gentleman.

I smile.

I step back slightly and turn around so that he can see the whole dress. It is a lot lower cut than I'd thought, and the sheer material barely covers the top of my butt.

When I come back around he is staring, slack-jawed, breathing heavier.

Desire flares in me again.

He extends his elbow to me, an offer, and I take it.

"Shall we?" he says.

"Yes." My voice sounds husky to my own ears. I want to stay at home tonight with him, but I know that won't happen.

Andrew and Red are waiting for us when we emerge into the hallway, both of them dressed in black tuxedos with matching bow ties. Red is holding my jacket, but Mikah quickly takes it from him. He opens it up and presents it to me to put my arms in, and I do.

He offers me his elbow once again, and we're off down the hall toward the elevator.

THIRTY-THREE

After a short drive in the limo we arrive at the Millennium Hotel downtown. Outside are people standing around and what seems like a never-ending stream of flashbulbs going off. Press? Photographers? Why?

Then I see the bright red carpet that extends from the street into the hotel.

"Take a deep breath, Vivienne, you look beautiful."

I do as Mikah has asked and I feel calmer almost instantly.

"Good job. All you have to do is stay close and smile. I will handle the rest."

I nod, not sure of my voice right now.

Red is at Mikah's door, and I see Connor coming down the carpet to meet us. I would much rather have Andrew. Though I trust Connor, especially after today, I like Andrew better.

It's almost as if he's sensed my preference; instead of joining Red, Connor walks to the front of the car and Andrew gets out. I see them exchange some words, and Andrew comes around as Red opens the door.

Mikah steps gracefully out of the car, his long fingers buttoning up his jacket as he stands.

Then his hand comes back into the car, extended in invitation, and I take it, sliding across the bench seat. As I step out, Mikah is quick to wrap his arm around me to steady me.

He waves, and I hear people shouting his name. Through the wave of flashbulbs I try to focus on where I'm going and what I'm doing, but it's hard; all the flashing lights are disorienting.

"Breathe," Mikah says.

I take a deep breath and smile. He releases my waist in exchange for taking my hand. I would much rather be closer to him, but it's hard to walk that way. I follow him along the line of cameras down the red carpet. Red and Andrew are right next to us.

About halfway up, he leans into my ear. "We're going to pause, face left, smile, then turn around and do the same on the other side. Then we will go straight in."

"Okay," I say with a little more confidence.

Two more steps and he stops and turns left, his hand leaving mine and coming to rest on the small of my back. I smile, and a flurry of flashbulbs go off in my face. I find it hard to look straight ahead. After a couple of heartbeats, we turn around to face yet another onslaught of flashes and more people shouting his name.

After another heartbeat I hear Mikah say, "Okay, let's go."

We turn back toward the door and make our way into the hotel almost double-time. I'm blinking rapidly, trying to clear the dark spots in my vision.

"Good evening, Mr. Blake," a gentleman in full livery says. "Right this way."

He leads us toward a bank of elevators. The spots are slowly subsiding, but I don't really get a chance to look around at the entrance of the hotel.

We reach the elevators and someone else in full livery is standing inside, holding the door. We all step in, and the doors close.

I hear Mikah let out a huge breath. "Glad that's over," he says.

I giggle a bit. "That was awful," I say, and all three men laugh.

Mikah looks down at me. His eyes are a vibrant green tonight. He's excited about this for some reason. "You look gorgeous," he says and smiles warmly at me.

I nudge him with my shoulder. "You don't look too bad yourself," I say back, surprised by my momentary lack of filter.

He smiles wider. "Thank you, Ms. Callahan." Whoa, where'd that come from? But his eyes are alight with even more excitement at my words.

After a few more beeps the doors finally open into a reception area. Off to the left are several coat racks behind a table.

"May I take your coat?" he asks.

I nod, suddenly nervous.

I turn my back toward him as I undo the two buttons in the front. He gently slips the jacket from my shoulders. A shiver runs through me as his fingers gently stroke along my shoulder. He hands my jacket to the lady at the table, who takes it and hands him a ticket in return. Once the exchange is done, he grabs my hand and we turn around.

Ahead of us is a set of double doors and a sign overhead that reads *Ballroom* in gold lettering.

I notice very quickly that the majority of the guests in the ballroom ahead are wearing black. There are a couple of red and blue dresses scattered throughout, but Mikah and I are the only ones in white.

Mikah leads me into the ballroom, which is huge but not packed full of people. Round tables surround a small stage and dance floor, and I'm suddenly anxious; I have no clue how to dance. I secretly hope that Mikah won't ask me to.

We work our way through the crowd. There are waitresses walking around with trays of glasses full of what I think is champagne. Mikah stops one of them and takes a flute from the tray. "Would you please get the lady some cider?"

"Yes, sir," she says, and she heads off, making a beeline for a table at the far end that is covered in full glasses and champagne bottles.

"Thank you," I say to Mikah, and he looks down at me, a quizzical look on his face. "For the cider," I add.

"Of course. Don't want you to be thirsty." He smiles.

"Mikah." A woman's voice carries over the hum of conversation, and I turn my head in its direction. Walking toward us is a woman with medium blond hair, cut into a cute pixie style, and bright brown eyes. Her floor-length black dress shimmers in the light.

I look at Mikah, who raises his glass in her direction as she approaches.

"Hello, darling," she says and places her hands on his shoulders to gently kiss each of his cheeks. I watch in awe. "You look fabulous."

"So do you."

She looks expectantly at me.

"Sydney, this is Vivienne," Mikah says.

Recognition registers on her face and she smiles warmly at me. "Vivienne, it is a pleasure to finally meet you. I've heard a lot about you."

I'm at a loss, but Mikah doesn't miss a beat. "Vivienne, Sydney is my senior partner and my right hand. She's the reason I've been able to take these last couple of weeks off."

"Oh, hello." I smile and offer her my hand. "It's an honor to meet you."

She takes my hand and we shake.

I can feel the pride washing off of Mikah. I too am surprised by my own poise and confidence. It's not something I've ever had to do, but it seems to come naturally to me.

The waitress has returned with my cider. I take the glass from her.

"Likewise," Sydney says. "I will let the two of you mingle and I will see you at dinner."

"Thanks, Sydney," Mikah says, and she's off, just like that.

I can see by her confidence and the way she greets people along the way that she's very comfortable with who she is and what she's doing here.

I take a sip of my drink. It's good. Sweet, but not too sweet, and bubbly.

"Come 'ere, I'd like to show you something," he says.

THIRTY-FOUR

He guides me by the small of my back toward a room to our right. As we approach the doorway I can see that the room has a domed ceiling of glass and that there are tables scattered around the room.

When we enter, I notice that each table has something on it. I can see everything from bottles of wine to books to a computer, and then some of the tables just have signs on them.

"This is a silent action." Mikah pauses his steps and turns toward me. "All the items in this room have been donated by someone in attendance. So whatever the winning bid is on an item, that money all goes toward the charity for tonight's event."

"What is tonight's charity?" I ask, rather anxious to know.

He takes my hand and leads me to a small round table on the left-hand side of the room. Upon the table is a sign that reads:

The 5th Annual Hearts and Hands Charity Gala
Hearts and Hands is a charity specializing in helping battered women and their children.

Hearts and Hands is also the parent company for many women's shelters throughout Minnesota, including Hope House and Amber's Place right here in Minneapolis.

Tonight's event is sponsored by MSB Enterprises and MSBE International.

My eyes fill with tears. The overwhelming emotion I feel is beyond anything I've felt in a long time.

Mikah leans down. "Please, don't cry."

"Did you do this for me?" I say through the tears.

"I'd love to say that I did, but my company started this gala about five years ago. Hearts and Hands was the first - and remains the primary - charity that my company supports." He gets down on one knee so that he can look up into my eyes. "I brought you here tonight because I felt it was important for you to see that my caring for you extends beyond just helping you. I take pride in my company's sponsorship of not only this event, but at least two others throughout the year. However, tonight's event is the big one of the year and raises more than five million dollars for Hearts and Hands." He reaches up to wipe away a stray tear on my cheek and my heart flutters at his touch. "Every dollar raised tonight is matched by me." He takes a deep breath. "I also brought you here because I need someone to help me run and organize MSB's charity division. I'd like, in time, for that person to be you."

I'm speechless and, to say the least, freaked out by his proposal. "Mikah, I haven't a clue about any of this."

He smiles warmly. "I know. Which is why I made the offer for you to go back to school - to learn." It's all starting to make sense now. "Vivienne, you're a brilliant young woman and you deserve every opportunity I can give you. I'd love to see what you're truly capable of when you put your mind to something. I want to see your passion for something shine and carry you into doing something you will love. You don't have to answer tonight, but please tell me you'll think about it."

The idea of going back to school was so overwhelmingly exciting for me when he first mentioned it, and now that I see there is a real purpose behind it, the idea is even harder to resist. "I'll think about it," I say quietly.

"Good. Now, let's take a look."

He stands, takes my hand, and leads me over to the first table, where we look at each of the items being auctioned before moving on to the next table. It takes about ten minutes to make our way through the room. The stand-up display on the last table says *MSB* on it. I read it.

Portfolio review and adjustment provided by MSB on a portfolio size of up to $10 million.
   Estimated value: $100,000.00

I look down at the bid sheet. Up until now, the bids have been very impressive, ranging anywhere from five thousand to sixty thousand, but this one surprises me most. The current bid stands at ninety-five thousand dollars. I gape at it.

"Holy cow."

"I told you," Mikah breathes, and I look at his beautiful bright blue eyes. Once again they've shifted colors, though the green lingers around the edges. He gestures around the room. "Did you see anything you like?"

I nod. A couple of tables back, there is a cool iPad and a laptop that looks similar to Mikah's, but both the iPad and computer have a special matching design on them done in the most beautiful deep purple with a rose in gold inlay. The center of the rose is created by a jewel - a diamond, I think. The tag said that they were specially designed and donated by some businesswoman out of Phoenix, and I wonder if she was the reason for Mikah's trip.

"Which one?" he asks.

"The iPad."

He smiles. "I thought you might like that one. Let's go take a look."

He turns us back in that direction just as an announcement comes from the other room. "Dinner is served, ladies and gentlemen. If you would please take your seats." Ironically enough, my stomach growls.

We approach the table and look at the bid sheet. It is up to thirty-five thousand dollars, and my eyes go wide as Mikah writes something on the sheet.

"What are you doing?" I squeak.

I see him shake with laughter at my tone. "What does it look like?"

He stands up, and I look down at the bid sheet.

THIRTY-FIVE

4. Vivienne Callahan $50,000.00

"Jesus, Mikah, I don't have that kind of money."

"Sure you do. You have a credit card, remember." He has a shit-eating grin on his face as he says this.

"No, Mikah, that is your credit card-"

"And you're free to purchase what you want with it. I told you that."

"But-"

"Don't argue, please. It's for a good cause, and there is a chance that you won't win," he says, but the confidence in his voice tells me that the bid he placed for me will win.

I know I'm going to lose this argument, but I have to at least try to help him see where I'm coming from. "Mikah, it's too much. I don't even know how to use it, or spend that kind of money on it. Surely there are cheaper alternatives."

"Of course there are, but I would rather see it go to a charity than to some business that will only use the money to further their profits. Besides, that is a one-of-a-kind design. Just like you."

He smiles warmly at me and my heart melts, at which point I lose any and all will to argue.

"Alright," I say, relenting even while secretly hoping I'll lose the bid.

He smiles wider and brushes his hand through his hair. "Shall we eat?"

I nod, and off we go toward the throng of people finding their tables. Mikah leads us straight to ours. Sitting in front of the beautiful place settings - china plates, silverware and crystal goblets - are tent cards with our names on them: *Ms. Vivienne Callahan* and *Mr. Mikah Blake.*

He pulls my chair out for me and I take a seat.

"Thank you," I say as he helps me slide in.

Instead of taking his seat, he remains standing behind his chair. Slowly the other eight chairs at our table are claimed, though half of the remaining chairs are occupied by women while their men stand behind them or behind their own chairs. Finally Sydney arrives, but she doesn't sit down, and I notice with curiosity that no one is with her, though there seems to be an empty chair next to her.

Looking around the room, I notice it is the same at every table: The women are seated - talking with the other women at the tables and drinking champagne - while the men stand behind them. Beyond the tables is a wall of floor-to-ceiling windows hung with elegant white and red curtains that are tied back with gold ropes, allowing the Minneapolis skyline to complete the room. An amazing view.

I look back at the glasses in front of me; there are three. One has water in it, another other contains what looks like champagne, and the third remains empty. I've never had champagne before, but I'm not about to try it now.

I reach for my water glass and take a sip. As I'm returning the glass to its place on the table, Mikah leans down and whispers, "The other glass is cider." I look more closely, comparing mine to Mikah's. The color of the liquid in my glass is just a shade darker. I smile.

After just a couple more minutes, a very attractive older gentleman with speckles of gray in his otherwise black hair comes to the table and pulls out Sydney's chair. She takes her seat, and he heads to the podium on the stage just across the dance floor from our table. I notice now that we are in the very center of the room.

"Welcome, ladies and gentlemen, to the Fifth Annual Hearts and Hands Gala. My name is Gary Harper, and I will be your emcee for this evening." He pauses to take a drink of water. "I'd like to start off this evening with a few announcements. The silent auction is over in the atrium, to my left. The bidding will remain open through dinner, and we will announce all of the winners during dessert. In the center of your tables you will all see an empty vase. Please feel free to place tips for your waiters and waitresses inside these. All of your servers tonight are here as volunteers and they are donating all of their tips to Hearts and Hands, so please, tip them well." He takes another sip of his water. "Now, without further ado, please, gentlemen, take your seats. Dinner is served."

And just like that, seeming to come out of the woodwork, are lines of servers, many of them carrying four plates at a time. They all head straight toward their designated tables. I am first to be served: grilled chicken breast, some vegetables and a spaghetti-style pasta salad. Chicken is far from my favorite, but I highly doubt peanut butter and jelly sandwiches are on the menu tonight.

Mikah's plate comes next, followed by the rest of the table's. I'm surprised to see that everyone else at the table has a thick, round cut of beef with the same sides as mine. And then my heart warms as I realize that Mikah has made special arrangements just for me.

I lean in close to him. "Thank you," I breathe.

He leans toward me and places his hand on my lap. I take it, and he squeezes my fingers gently. "You're most welcome." He holds my hand long enough for me to begin to wonder how I'm going to eat one-handed, but then he squeezes again and lets go.

THIRTY-SIX

Gary comes down from the podium to join us, sitting next to Sydney and kissing her on the cheek. They make a beautiful couple. He smiles at me and begins to eat, just like the rest of us.

Mikah, Sydney and Gary make small conversation throughout the meal. I get about halfway through my chicken before my stomach starts to turn a little, so I stop eating the meat and focus instead on the vegetables and pasta salad. I eat everything else on my plate and put down my fork and knife.

"The chicken too much?" Mikah asks me quietly.

"It was really good, someone just has better ideas." I smile at his grin.

"I can ask for something else for you."

"No, I'm actually pretty full. But thank you."

"Okay. Are you feeling okay?" he asks.

"I'm good." I smile.

"Let me know if that changes, okay?" he says, his tone sincere.

"I will."

He goes back to finishing up his meal. I notice that tonight, like most nights, he cleans his plate.

I watch as people get up and begin milling about. Many walk toward the silent auction or over toward the bar at the back of the room. Some stand around talking to people at other tables. A couple of times people come and speak with Mikah or Sydney, or both. I don't pay much attention to most of their conversation, as it is business-related.

As more and more people finish eating, the dull murmur in the room increases to a roar. Gary takes this as his cue and excuses himself from the table, heading toward the stage. Rather than stand on it, he grabs the microphone and says, "Ladies and gentlemen, the silent auction will be closing in five minutes."

Panic sets in; I hope and pray that someone else has outbid me. I couldn't even bring myself to look at the price tag of the purse I bought yesterday; how on earth am I going to manage paying fifty thousand dollars for something?

My stomach churns, more from nerves than anything, I hope, and I notice Mikah looking at me. "What?" I say quietly.

He grins. "Nothing. You're just so beautiful."

On cue I blush.

Then I move to stand up, and Mikah, along with all the remaining men at the table, do the same.

"Where are you going?" he asks, concerned.

"The ladies' room."

I can see the silent "Oh" on his face. "Are you alright?" he whispers.

I smile. "Yes, I just need to use the restroom."

He offers me his hand. "I'll show you."

I know where they are - I saw them when we walked in - but it's not worth the argument. I take his hand and he leads me between the tables back toward the entrance.

For the first time all evening, I notice Red and Andrew standing near the door. I take strange comfort in knowing they're here, and I smile at them as we pass.

Mikah escorts me right up to the bathroom door, and I step inside. The bathroom is just as elegant as the rest of the ballroom, with gold accents everywhere.

A couple minutes later I emerge, having freshened up just a bit. Mikah immediately takes my hand again and we head back toward the ballroom. Gary is back onstage, organizing pieces of paper - no doubt the auction bids - and my stomach rolls again.

On our way back to our table, Mikah stops to make small talk with some of the guests. He introduces me to most of them, and I hope there won't be a test; I can't keep them all straight.

Then Gary takes up the microphone and asks everyone to return to their seats. Mikah and I head over that way to find that our desserts are already on the table. It's some tan-colored pudding; it almost looks like caramel or butterscotch. I'm suddenly eager to find out.

Again, Mikah is a gentleman, pulling my chair out for me and helping me scoot in. This time, though, he doesn't wait before he, too, takes his seat.

Just as he sits down there is a flurry of bubbles in my belly, in the same area as yesterday, and my hand flies to the spot.

Mikah is quick to notice the shift in my posture. He leans in. "Are you okay?"

I smile wide. I don't respond, but I grab his hand and pull it toward my bump. His eyes widen as he realizes what I'm about to do.

I gently push his palm against my stomach. His hand is huge - it covers nearly the entire lower half of my bump - and I can feel the heat from his skin radiating through my dress.

Nothing happens. I remember that yesterday when I applied more pressure she moved again, so I press his hand a little tighter against my bump and look at him.

He seems confused, like he can't feel anything, which is understandable because she hasn't moved again.

Gary is talking at the podium, but I can't stop staring into Mikah's eyes. I'm lost in them. Consumed by his beautiful gaze. I pull his hand in a little tighter, and just like that, the bubbles return.

Mikah looks down and then back up at me, his expression changing from confusion to wonder. His eyes are alight with excitement as the bubbles continue for a few more beats, and then they are welling up with tears.

I reach up and gently cup his cheek. He kisses my palm as I do and then leans into my touch. The bubbles have stopped, but I can tell he doesn't want to move his hand, and I'm not sure I want him to, either. I place my right hand over his on my belly and pull my other hand away from his cheek. I can't be sure, but I think he actually pouts briefly.

THIRTY-SEVEN

Gary is talking about how Hearts and Hands has grown over the last fifteen years, and with each passing year they are able to help more and more women leave abusive relationships.

"This year alone, Amber's Place has taken in more than two hundred women, and each and every one of them have either found jobs or are seeking stable employment and stable places to live.

"Currently there are more than twenty thousand women in Minneapolis alone that are living in abusive relationships. With this year's gala, Hearts and Hands hopes to expand Amber's Place to accommodate another one hundred women and their children, bringing the total up to two hundred and twenty-two rooms.

"Women who visit Amber's place are allowed to stay as long as they need to in order to obtain a job and to secure housing and financial assistance from the state to get them started and on their way to a better and brighter future.

"Tonight, we are proud to welcome four women, our guests of honor, who were once residents of Amber's Place."

Am I one of these women here tonight?

"Ladies and gentleman, please give a warm round of applause to Sydney Harper, my wife and Vice President of MSB Enterprises."

Whoa, what?

I watch as Sydney stands, tears in her eyes, and makes her way to the podium. She hugs Gary, then she stands beside him and begins to speak. "Thank you, Gary, and thank you, ladies and gentlemen, for your generous support tonight. I would also like to recognize the three other women who are guests with us here tonight, though I will not name them as I have been named.

"I knocked on Amber's door about seven years ago. I had just walked out - with my daughter, who is now eight - of a physically and emotionally abusive relationship. One day, after hearing about Hearts and Hands, I found the strength to walk away.

"When I arrived at Amber's Place, I was bruised and battered, but I was welcomed with open arms. Once I was inside the safety of their walls, and through their encouragement, I was able to call the police and have charges pressed against my attacker.

"Had it not been for Amber's Place and their willingness to help me get back on my feet, I would never have been able to find a job that put my hard-earned degree to good use. I am forever thankful to Mikah Blake and his staff for their support and endless patience when I began to learn the ropes."

I immediately understand all the pieces of who Mikah is and the things that he's done for me and it becomes clear that this is who he is.

"It is through strong will and determination that I stand here before you today. The idea behind Hearts and Hands is to give the women who go there a real chance at life, to give them a fresh start not only in their jobs but with themselves, as well.

"I am proud to tell you that tonight's event has been our most successful ever. We have raised three million, two hundred and twenty-one thousand dollars. I am also honored to be a part of MSB, who will be matching every dollar raised for a grand total of six million, four hundred and forty-two thousand dollars."

Mikah's hand comes away from my belly, as does mine, and we join the rest of the guests in a standing ovation.

The tears overwhelm my eyes as reality hits me. I'm one of those two hundred women who've been through Amber's Place this year. Two hundred is such a small number when compared to the thousands still out there suffering. How can I even begin to say no to Mikah's offer to help me become a part of their solution?

The applause continues as I gently wipe away the tears that have spilled from my eyes. Mikah hands me his handkerchief, and I take it. He wraps his arm around my back and pulls me close.

I look up at him, and he is looking at me, his eyes full of emotion.

"Yes," I say.

He cocks his head to one side.

"Yes, I'll work for you. I'll go to school. Whatever it is you want me to do, I'll do it."

He smiles, wide and bright, and pulls me in tighter to kiss my forehead. Once again, I'm left with a strong desire to kiss him.

The applause finally dies down. Gary has taken back the microphone.

"Does Sydney know about me?" I ask Mikah as he helps me to sit once again. I expect him to say yes, but he doesn't; he shakes his head.

Once Sydney has returned to the table, Mikah sits back down. I'm in awe of her speech and her openness about having been a victim of domestic violence.

Mikah leans in and whispers in my ear, "I thought it would be more appropriate if it came from you. That is a part of your life, and it is your story to tell, not mine."

I reach for his hand and squeeze, my silent reassurance that I've heard him. My heart swells at the overwhelming amount of respect I now have for him.

THIRTY-EIGHT

Gary begins announcing the winners of the silent auction. I'm thankful that the dollar amounts are not being announced. Mikah and I have been holding hands between each announcement and the clapping that follows. My palms are starting to turn red.

Gary seems to be going in random order, so I'm completely surprised when it has been some time since it began and neither Mikah's donated lot nor the one he so graciously bid on have been announced yet. But given that Mikah's was by far the highest valued item, it would make sense if Gary saved until last.

"And now, for our second-to-last item of the evening, we have our Escaping with Technology package. Donated and designed by CTM Capital out of Phoenix, Arizona, this item contains an iPod, an iPad, and a MacBook Pro laptop, all inlaid with various gems and fully loaded with business-grade software. The package also includes more than one thousand dollars in gift cards, a set of matching bags and cases, and ten hours of tutoring time, and it is valued at more than seventy-five thousand dollars."

I'm not sure I can breathe right now. I look at Mikah, who is looking at me with the biggest cat-ate-the-canary expression on his face.

"And the winner of this impressive package is..." Dramatic pause. Does he not know that I can't breathe right now? "Ms. Vivienne Callahan."

The entire room erupts in applause. Mikah is clapping and staring at me. My mouth drops open and I feel like a fish out of water, fighting to suck in air in order to breathe.

When the applause finally dies down, Mikah's still looking self-satisfied, but there is a warmth about it, too. "Way to go," he says.

Seriously? Did he seriously just say that? "I'm kind of angry with you right now," I say through gritted teeth.

He leans back dramatically, pretending to be appalled, and I cannot help but laugh at his expression. He smiles back, leans over, and places his arm along the back of my chair. His hand begins to play with a strand of my hair. "Please don't be angry. I would not have made a bid of that size if it wasn't alright. Okay?"

Gah! Why does he do this? "I feel guilty for using your money."

"Don't. It's alright. And besides, it will help you with school." He smirks at me, but the reminder that I've agreed to go to school and help him with the charity work makes me feel excited again.

Bubbles flit in my belly as the baby moves around once more, and I tense, just a little.

Mikah notices. "What's wrong?"

I smile wide at him and he knows.

"Again?"

I nod.

He smiles as Gary announces the winner of Mikah's donated lot and the room applauds.

Mikah pulls his hand back and we both join in.

"Ladies and gentlemen, thank you again for coming and for your generous support of Hearts and Hands. Please be sure to see the table in the auction room to claim your winnings, and enjoy the band." The room applauds once more, and the band that I hadn't notice set up behind us starts to play.

"Dance with me?" Mikah says.

Oh, no. My worst fear of tonight, aside from the auction, is being realized. He wants to dance.

I look at him, no doubt with overwhelming fear in my eyes, but his expression is warm and soft.

"It's easy, come on."

He stands, pulls my chair back from the table, and offers me his hand. Instinct sets in and I take it.

I look at the dance floor. There are already several couples dancing, which instantly makes me feel better; at least I won't be on display. Well, not the center of it, anyway.

"I don't know how to dance," I say as he takes me in his arms.

"It's easy, just follow my lead."

I position my hands like his and he starts off slowly, left to right, and then he's off.

The gentle pressure against my back and squeezes of my hand tell me what direction he is going to go, and all in all, it's not that bad. I'm not going to win any trophies for dancing, but it is fun just the same.

THIRTY-NINE

About halfway through our second song, my back comes alive with a zinging fire. Mikah, too, stiffens, and we stop dancing. He's looking around rather frantically, searching for something.

That's when I see it. Over at the door, near where we came in, a man is trying to come inside, but he is quickly headed off by Andrew and Red. They are pushing him back and away from door toward the elevators.

"Mikah," I say and nod my head in the direction of the door.

He turns to see. "Shit," he growls.

"What's going on? Who is that?"

"Come on. Come with me."

He takes my hand and we head toward the hall opposite the emcee's stage. There are several other people standing there, so we don't look out of place, but that doorway is our only way out.

We're out of the intruder's line of sight and well-hidden behind a rather large planter. I'm pressed up against Mikah, and I feel a vibration in his pocket.

He reaches his hand in and pulls out his phone. "Yeah." His tone is clipped. "Make sure he is gone off of the property, and we will wrap things up here. Send

Andrew back up to escort us down." He pauses. "Are we sure he was alone?" He listens. "Yeah, okay. Thanks, Red."

He pulls the phone away from his ear. "It's time to go."

"Mikah, what's going on? Who was that?" There was something about that man that was familiar, but I couldn't place him. He was dressed up in a tux and looked like he belonged here with the others.

"We're going to square away your auction winnings, say good-bye to Sydney and take off. I don't know about you, but I'm tired."

I grip his arm tightly and pull him back toward me. He leans down slightly so that we are eye to eye and I don't have to talk loudly. "Don't you dare shelter me, Mikah. Who in the hell was that man?"

I see resolve in his features. He doesn't want to tell me. But then something changes and he leans in a little closer to me.

"That was Elton Bennett."

FORTY

"Riley's father?" is all I can manage to whisper.

"Yes. He is an ex-business partner of mine. Our ties were severed the minute I discovered who was after you. My staff has done a pretty damn good job of damaging his reputation. He's pissed and wants revenge on me."

"Does he know about me, who I am?" I'm trying to wrap my brain around all of this.

Mikah takes a deep breath. "He knows of Vivienne Callahan, but I don't know that he is aware that you are her. He may or may not make the connection. I'm guessing by your reaction you didn't know him, either?"

I shake my head. "No. Riley never introduced me to his father." I don't go into the reasons why that is with Mikah, but I think Riley's words were that I wasn't good enough for the upper class and that I was "a good-for-nothing whore." I shiver at the memory but move past it quickly.

Mikah turns as someone approaches. "Hi, Sydney."

"Hello, you two. Vivienne, I would like to thank you so much for your generous bid and to congratulate you on winning," she says. She is very friendly, awkwardly so.

I smile. "It was really Mikah's doing."

164

She smiles, bright and warm, giving me the distraction I need from what has just happened. "I know. I saw the handwriting."

She and I both laugh. Mikah has a look of mock disgust on his face, and we laugh a little harder.

"Either way, thank you. And thanks for coming." She takes me by the shoulders and kisses each of my cheeks. "I look forward to seeing you again." She steps back and turns toward Mikah. "Will you be in on Monday?"

He looks down at me and shrugs. "Let's see how the weekend goes."

She smiles. "Sounds good to me. Enjoy your evening." She waves and heads back toward Gary.

Mikah leads me toward the table that now separates the two rooms.

"Good evening, Mr. Blake," the elderly woman behind the table says.

"Hello. This-" His long fingers casually gesture in my direction. "-is Vivienne Callahan. She-"

"Oh, of course. Thank you so much, Ms. Callahan, for your bid and your donation." She stands and turns to a gentleman behind her, and he goes toward the tables where the last few remaining prizes are sitting. There is a beautiful deep purple case on the table with the same rose pattern on it as the laptop.

"How would you like to make your donation tonight, Ms. Callahan?" the elderly woman asks.

I look to Mikah briefly, trying desperately not to look completely freaked out.

Mikah smiles and turns to the woman. "Credit card."

"Perfect," she says and reaches for something on a table behind her.

I reach into my purse, glad that I didn't take the credit card out of my wallet when I switched bags this afternoon. I pull it out and hand it to her. She does a couple of things and hands me a receipt and a pen. Having just done this for the first time yesterday with Celeste, I'm suddenly thankful for the shopping spree. I sign my name with a shaky hand and give her back the receipt and pen.

"Wonderful, you're all set," she says as the gentlemen hands me the case. Mikah grabs it before I can and slings it over his shoulder.

"Thanks so much for all your help this evening," he says to both of them, and off we go toward the door.

Andrew is waiting with my coat in hand. Mikah takes it from him and offers it to me. I turn, slip my arms inside and quickly button it as Andrew hits the call button on the elevator.

The doors open immediately and we step inside.

FORTY-ONE

We make it to the limo in what feels like record time, helped by the fact that the reporters and photographers who were here when we arrived are gone now. I also note that, though the windows are up, every light in the back half of the limo is on.

"Thank you for a fabulous evening," I say once we are settled and in motion.

He looks at me, tenderness in his eyes. "You're most welcome, Vivienne. I had a wonderful time."

I slide a little closer to him and he wraps his arm around me, holding me close.

Sitting here next to him, after seeing Elton in the ballroom, I realize how safe I feel. I know that, no matter what, he will protect me from anything and everything that can be thrown at me. Even though Riley is still out there and the possibility of his finding me sends a chill through me, what Zirah said about Riley's fate has me feeling more and more certain that Riley will likely never be coming after me again. I'm finally starting to see that over the last couple of weeks my mind, too, has been healing, and Mikah is responsible for that.

I'm also hyperaware of the fact that the feelings I have for Mikah in the dream are becoming reality.

"I'm sorry that I ever accused you of bad intentions when you offered to help me," I say quietly. He pulls back a little and I look up at him. He's puzzled. "In the hospital. Well, the first time we were there. Every time I've jumped to conclusions, I've been wrong, and I apologize."

He takes a deep, thinking-style breath. "You had every right to think and even express those things. I realize now that I came at you pretty strongly without knowing your circumstances." He smiles slightly. "So for that, I apologize."

"You're forgiven," I whisper as I snake my arms around him and hug him tight.

He lets out a breathy chuckle. "Thank you for your forgiveness and..." He pauses long enough for me to pull back and look up at him expectantly. His eyes are soft, filled with something I'm not sure I recognize. "I don't know how to express to you what it meant to me tonight, when she was moving around. I've never felt anything like that before. It was..." He doesn't add anything more to that statement, but I know what he's trying to say.

I lean back into him, and a sudden vision fills my mind: Mikah with a beautiful baby girl with curly red hair. Though this baby is not his biologically, he feels some deeper connection to her than I ever could have expected from anyone.

The idea of Mikah stepping into her life as someone she can look up to brings new tears to my eyes. I succeed in blinking them back so that they don't drip onto his shirt. I don't want him to know what I'm thinking about right now.

We pull into the underground garage and are met by Connor at the elevators. He opens Mikah's door, and

Mikah slips out. I follow right behind him when he offers his hand again.

We ride up with Connor and Red in the elevator. Their presence makes me a little nervous because they don't usually ride with us. But after tonight's events with Elton and this morning's events with the shifter, their caution is understandable.

Jeez, could today have been any more of a mess?

FORTY-TWO

After I've washed my face and changed into one of Mikah's t-shirts, I stand in the doorway watching him work on his laptop. I notice that my iPod is playing quietly in the background and the TV is off.

He's rid himself of his jacket, vest and tie. I can't see if he's changed his pants, but he is still wearing his dress shirt, so I think not.

"You don't have to stand back there and watch me," he says, surprising me. "Come here."

I smirk, totally busted. I push away from the doorway and walk around the couch. He puts down whatever it is that he's been looking at and opens up his arms.

I go stand between his legs, and he puts his hands on the backs of my thighs. When he gently rests his head against the upper curve of my bump, that surge of desire returns. Once again the urge to kiss him comes over me, this time stronger than before, nearly overpowering.

Though he hasn't actually made any moves toward advancing our relationship, he's shown me no reason to fear rejection. On the contrary, everything he's done tells me that he needs me, too.

I run my hand through his hair and he holds me tighter, closer to him. When he does this I'm instantly reminded of the dream - our dream - and how he took so much care in preparing my outfit for tonight. He, too, must feel and see the same things as I do in that dream.

"Are you ready for bed?"

I yawn. "Yes."

I step back, and it's there in his eyes - that look I saw earlier - and in this context it strikes me as desire.

I take his head in my hands and lean down. He doesn't flinch or say anything. But as I move my lips closer to his face, fear washes over me, and I end by kissing him on his forehead.

"Good night, Mikah. Thank you for a wonderful evening."

"Good night, beautiful. You're most welcome, and I'm very glad you were there with me." He smiles. "See you in the morning."

I nod and head off toward bed.

FORTY-THREE

I'm back in the white room. Mikah is down on his knees with his eyes closed, wings fully extended. It's right where we left off the last time I had this dream, and here I have no inhibitions about doing anything to him.

I reach up and place my palm against his face. He leans into my touch. "Give me your hand," I say, and he does. I bring it up past my face and place it on the top of my wing. Pleasure surges through me, hot and rapid, pooling between my thighs.

I take his head in both my hands, and he mirrors the gesture on my own cheeks.

He rises, bringing me with him, tilting my head upwards. I feel my belly bump into him, pressing gently into his stomach. His eyes open, and they are the purest blue I could ever imagine.

Steadily, he brings his face closer to mine. The motion is impossibly slow and I ache with anticipation. I stretch upward a little in an attempt to meet him faster, and he smiles.

Just like that, his lips are on mine. All my angst and anguish dissolve in an instant, and I'm lost to the soft, warm touch of his lips.

His tongue lightly traces the outline of my lips, teasing me, tempting me to open them. Desperate to feel his tongue on mine, I open my mouth. The touch is electric. It surges, hard and hot, straight to my innermost desires of love and lust.

Desire. He's awakened a need stronger than anything I've ever felt before.

His kiss grows more urgent, and his hands move slowly and lightly down my neck to my shoulders and then along my arms. I shiver at the contact from wanton need.

My nipples, which are already tight and tender, harden and ache. An ache that can only be soothed by something warm and wet.

His fingers trail back up my arms as my hands slowly slide down his neck, along his chest, then follow the line of his ribs. I bring my arms around him, desperate to be closer to him, to be touching him.

His ragged breathing matches mine. We're both practically gasping for air as our kiss deepens. Nothing else matters; there is nothing in the world but him and me. Us.

A loud grunt. It comes from behind me and is followed by a moan, but it is not from me or Mikah. It's something else...

"Ahh."

This is real, different. It's not my dream. I'm awake, and someone is moaning, but not in pain.

"Mmmm."

My eyes fly open. There is light in the room, but from where? I sit up and look behind me, thinking it's the bathroom, but no, it's coming from the corner, near the closet door.

It's.... What is that?

"Ahh!" it comes again.

I jump to my feet and turn around. My eyes are adjusting to the light. It's not bright, but I can see now that it is coming from the kitchen, but at a very strange angle.

My hand flies to my mouth. "Holy shit," I mumble.

I pull my hand away and take a deep breath.

It's Mikah. He's on his knees on the kitchen floor. But that's not what has my attention. Spread out in full, awesome splendor are a pair of brilliantly white wings.

FORTY-FOUR

I walk quietly toward him. I can't tell if he's awake or sleeping. He's not looking at me, but down toward the floor. As I get closer I see his wings flare and twitch slightly.

When I'm about five steps away from him, I shed my shirt so that I'm down to my bra and lacy boy shorts. I don't want to destroy his shirt.

I concentrate extra hard and, after a beat, I feel them pushing out, spreading outward. The sensation is strange, almost like arms emerging from my body. I smile at the fact that I was able to bring them out on my own.

Once I feel as though they are fully extended, I open my eyes and peer over my shoulder. They are as brilliant as they were this morning, but bigger, and I gasp as I watch them shimmer in the faint light of the kitchen.

I test the muscles in my back, flexing them. My wings move slightly and a thrill of excitement washes over me.

I turn back toward Mikah. He hasn't moved, but his breathing has grown strained, ragged like in the dream.

I take the five small steps I need to reach him and stop.

I reach down and gently stroke the stubble along his jaw. He leans into my touch. I lower myself to my knees; they slide along his as they come to rest on the floor.

"Keep your eyes closed," I whisper.

He nuzzles into my touch a shade more, and with my other hand, eager to see if the sensation is the same, I reach for his wing. When I make contact, his mouth goes slack, his breathing stops momentarily, and the feathers of his wings flare. He moans: a warm, sensual sound.

I pull my hand back and cup the other side of his face. He does the same with my face.

"Kiss me," I breathe, and he rises up, bringing me with him.

I'm looking up at him, and slowly, even more slowly than in the dream, he lowers his kiss to mine. I stretch, hoping to meet his mouth faster, and he smiles.

The next thing I know, his lips are on mine, soft and warm, hot and needy. The moment we make contact, satisfaction and desire sweep through me. I can feel his need in the touch of his lips, in the trembling of his fingers against my face, a need that matches my own.

His tongue lightly teases my lips. I part them. In an instant, his tongue is on mine, teasing and tasting.

My hands slide along his neck, down his sternum, and then follow his ribs. I slip my arms around him, bringing him closer and tighter against me. His chest touches mine. My belly presses into his taut stomach and his hands trail along my neck, shoulders and arms.

I shiver, causing all my nerve endings to come alive.

Sliding my hands up his back, I find the tips of the feathers on the bottom of his wings and I lightly stroke them. His erection comes to life against my belly. I moan into his mouth as my eyes roll back into my head.

I open my eyes again and he is looking at me. His bright blue eyes are warm, filed with need and with something else, that emotion that I can't quite name.

Then, confusion.

He pulls back, trying to gain his bearings, unsure of where he is. The vision in front of him hits him. I can tell the moment that he realizes that my wings are spread wide. He flexes his shoulders, and his eyes grow wider still as he understands that his wings are open and visible, too.

"How..."

"The dream. We've..." I take a deep breath, trying hard to calm my breathing. "We've been sharing the same dreams."

He sits back on his feet, but he doesn't release the grip he now has on my hands.

"Mikah, I want this. I want you," I say breathlessly.

He doesn't need any more encouragement from me. He stands, steadying himself as he realizes the full weight of his upper body with his wings fully emerged. He pulls me up by my hands and I stand with him. He's quick to cup my face, and once again his lips are on mine.

His kiss is urgent and my body responds, desire pooling stronger deep inside of me. I put everything I have into our kiss, pulling him tighter and closer against me, and he does the same. I feel his fingers weave into my hair as he gently urges me to take a step back. I do, and he nudges again. And again. I refuse to open my eyes as he continues to urge me backwards; I'm completely lost to his kiss, his lips, his hands in my hair.

Then I feel the bed against my knees and I stop. His kisses wander from my mouth to my jaw, behind my ear, down my neck, along my shoulder, his lips soft against my skin, leaving a trail of blazing hot nerves in their wake.

His hands glide down my body along the outside swell of my breasts, down my ribs. Feather light, his fingers trail the sweet curves of my bump, and I'm lost to the purest pleasure I've ever felt in my life.

His kisses continue, and the need to have him grows hotter, stronger. My legs begin to tremble, but still he runs his hands up my back toward my wings, and I shiver in anticipation of his touch along my feathers. But he stops when he reaches the clasp of my bra.

He pauses, waiting for permission.

"Yes," I breathe.

His breathing spikes. He shakes slightly, as though nervous, but he hasn't stopped his kisses along the swell of my breasts. I raise my hand to his hair and run my fingers through its soft texture. It tickles against my palm.

With my fingers I urge him to pull back slightly. He does so and looks at me. His eyes are hooded with desire and something deeper, some stronger emotion trying desperately to spill through.

"I. Want. You." I emphasize each word. "I'm ready."

"I...I don't know if I am," he whispers.

"What do you mean?" I cock my head toward him.

He sinks to his knees in front of me, looking into my eyes with an intensity that's almost frightening. "If we cross this line, everything changes. We-" He swallows. "I will never be able to be apart from you. Everything between us will be different."

I sit down on the bed. Then I reach my hands around my back, reaching for the clasp of my bra. As I unhook each tiny hook, one at a time, he watches me, eyes wide but excited.

Finally I reach the last one and I look at him, pleading with my eyes, trying to show him just how much I need him. We're face to face, and as I unhook the last of the clasps, I bring my arms tight against my sides so as not to allow my bra to completely fall away.

I bring my hands back around to cup his face.

"I'm tired of fighting the urge to kiss you." I lean in and kiss him. Softly, gently. "I'm no longer able to resist being closer to you. I can't stand that we sleep in separate rooms, or that I feel as though I can't touch you." I splay my right hand wide and run the tips of my fingers down his beautiful face from his forehead to his chin. As I reach his lips they part, and I feel his hot breath caress my hand.

"Bring our dream to life. Show me that you cannot resist me." I straighten my arms, pull them away from my body, and let my bra fall down, fully exposing my breasts. The cool air hardens my nipples further.

I hear his sharp intake of breath. "You are so beautiful. An angel. My angel."

He reaches up to cup my face and brings his lips to mine. I feel him push forward, pushing me onto my back, and by some miracle, I manage to pull my wings in as he lays me back on the bed.

He hovers over me, the skin of his tight stomach gently touching mine as our lips continue their slow, sensual assault, lighting up my senses.

He trails his fingers down my neck, along my chest, across my nipple. I moan as the ache is relieved by his touch. He continues down my ribs to my stomach, and the sweet touch along my bump once again sends delicious shivers through my body.

He begins to kiss me along the same path his hand has just taken, and goose bumps begin to radiate across my skin.

I'm lost to my desire.

Acknowlegements

THANK YOU!! From the bottom of my heart I cannot thank you all enough for your amazing support!

I'd like to first thank my editor - Sione. Your patience and unyielding words of encouragement mean the world to me. Thank you for all your amazing hard work and dedication to this project.

My Son deserves so much credit here! He puts up with Mommy writing, Mommy stressed out, and without that patience, I wouldn't have been able to finish this project.
My Mom - I love you with all my heart! Your support and encouragement knows no end. Thank you for everything you've done.

Barb, Rachel, and Vickie - Girls, you sure do know how to keep me on track, your subtle and not so subtle hints are well received, I'm working on it, I promise!!

The Z-TEAM!! I HEART YOU GUYS!! Your love of my writing is inspiring and I look forward to many more adventures with your guys!

To my fans and friends - I HEART YOU ALL SOOOO HUGE!!

Thank you Thank You THANK YOU!!

Find More Zoey

On Twitter: www.twitter.com/ZoeyDerrick
On Facebook: www.facebook.com/Zoey.Derrick.1 -
Personal
www.facebook.com/Zoey.Derrick (Author)
On Her Website: www.ZoeyDerrick.com
Email Her: Zoey@ZoeyDerrick.com
Amazon Author Page: Find it Here

Other Works By Zoey Derrick

Finding Love's Wings

CAMERON ENDERS seems to have it all: a brand new condo in a city she loves, a top executive position at an international entertainment firm, an insane amount of money, and a gorgeous boyfriend. But when Cami catches the boyfriend in the act with another woman, it triggers all the anguish from years of neglect by her parents, and she realizes she never learned how to love or be loved. Cami flees to the remote tropical island of Tarah, but she can't avoid facing her problems any longer when she meets the man of her fantasies...

TRISTAN MICHAELS, one of Hollywood's hottest new stars, has come to Tarah to ride out a storm. His girlfriend of five years has been caught on camera cheating, and she's determined to make Tristan stop the story from breaking. But Tristan's done cleaning up her messes. He needs to escape all things Hollywood for a while--and especially the firm that represents him--until the whole thing blows over. What he doesn't count on is meeting an irresistibly beautiful woman, a woman who just so happens to be the CEO of the firm he's trying to avoid.

Can Tristan and Cami help each other learn to trust and love again, or will their histories of betrayal tear them apart?
This story contains Tattoos, Piercings, a Hot Movie Star and a Sexy Heroine. No rich guy poor girl story here, just a story of what it's like to learn to love.

The Struggle
27 writers. 29 original stories and poems. A single theme:
The Struggle.

Proceeds from the sale of this anthology will go to helping writers in need.

From horror and humor to love and loss, each tale reflects the struggles we all have to face – in life, and within ourselves. They are as varied as the array of talent who united to create them, spinning the threads of storytelling together to weave an extraordinary anthology unlike any other.

The Struggle features works by Delilah S. Dawson, Michael Birchmore, Bobby Salomons, Sue Birchmore, James R. Tuck, Corey Seeley, Sheila Hall, Lily Luchesi, Karina Cooper, Mari Wells, Andrea Wheeler, Sarah Broadley, J. Luis Licea, Zoey Derrick, Aly Morlock, Casey Harris-Parks, Samantha Lee, Trevor Neale, J. Elizabeth Hill, Romantic Dominant, J. Hewitt, Christopher Liccardi,

GIVE ME DESIRE - REASON SERIES #3

Caroline Rainbow, Gabi Daniels, Peter Davis-Parker, and Rick Austin.

About Zoey

Amazon Best Selling Angels, Demons & Devils and Paranormal Author of Give Me Reason - The Reason Series Book One comes from Glendale, Arizona. Zoey, was a mortgage underwriter by day and is now a paranormal, romance and erotica novelist full-time. She writes stories as hot as the desert sun itself. It is this passion that drips off of her work, bringing excitement to anyone who enjoys a good and sensual love story.

Not only does she aim to take her readers on an erotic dance that lasts the night, it allows her to empty her mind of stories we all wish were true.
Her stories are hopeful yet true to life, skillfully avoiding melodrama and the unrealistic, bringing her gripping Erotica only closer to the heart of those that dare dipping into it.

The intimacy of her fantasies that she shares with her readers is thrilling and encouraging, climactic yet full of suspense. She is a loving mistress, up for anything, of which any reader is doomed to return to again and again

www.ingramcontent.com/pod-product-compliance
Lightning Source LLC
Chambersburg PA
CBHW050939120626
46552CB00001B/285